To Take A Wife
(To Have Not To Hold)

As realised by
SJ Hills.

A fresh new drama based on the classic Restoration Comedy *The Country Wife* by Wycherley, famously banned from print for over 200 years and considered too outrageous to be performed at all.

A Ribaldry Tale Of Insatiable Lust and Social Consequences
From the author of *Scarborough Fair* and *Wishing Well*

This Work First Published In 2009
by Century17 Publishing, London.
www.century-17.com

This paperback edition first published in 2009

Typeset in Times New Roman by Century17 Publishing.

First Edition. Revision I. I-III-V
ISBN 978-0-9559921-2-4

Century17 Publishing
Restoring classics from the past
Rewriting classics for the future

PREFACE

Mr Horner is a bachelor with a reputation as a lady's man. In order to up the quality of his conquests and gain uninhibited access to previously forbidden society households, he concocts a rumour that an accident during a recent trip to France has robbed him of his manhood. A previously untried, unproven and somewhat unorthodox ploy to satisfy his carnal desires.

Mr Pinchwife, a notorious womaniser in his younger days, has taken the safe option of marrying a very young, innocent country wife as he 'can't keep a whore in town'. He knows the ways of the town and is driven to distraction trying to keep his wife from the attentions of the town rakes.

After a chance meeting when her husband brings her to London to attend her sister-in-law's wedding (to further her position in society), Mr Horner decides Mrs Pinchwife is a challenge he cannot resist. Can he corrupt and bed the young impressionable country wife despite her husband's constant vigil, and can he persuade the society ladies of London, whose reputations must be upheld at all costs, to succumb to his attentions?

In the notorious 'china shop' scene, Horner makes love to a woman while her husband stands outside the door encouraging her exploits, believing she is being chastised by the 'incapable' Horner for mischievous behaviour, hinting at sexual practices considered depraved at the time.

To Take A Wife is an adaptation by SJ Hills of the notorious drama *The Country Wife,* written by Wycherly in 1675. Often referred to as 'the smuttiest play ever written', famously banned from print for over 200 years, and considered too outrageous to be performed at all. (David Garrick's cleaned up version, *The Country Girl*, was performed in place of the original until recent, more enlightened times.)

While losing none of the appeal of the original work, this is a completely new work, rewritten from the ground up, tying up ambiguous elements in the original storyline, bringing each thread together more effectively for the final dramatic conclusion, and adding elements to make it enjoyable for modern day readers, players and audience alike, yet still remaining timeless.

Packed full of witty dialogue, innuendo, society one-upmanship, and copious helpings of bawdiness, the infamous drama is given a fresh new life.

As Covent Garden still exists today almost unchanged, one can experience the feel of the drama by visiting the cobbled streets, the opera house, the pubs, the street performers and the market stalls, as does the author on regular occasions.

Titles by SJ Hills.

Scarborough Fair.
> (Restoration Comedy style drama based on *The Relapse* by Vanbrugh –
> considered too risqué to be performed for over 200 years)

To Take A Wife.
> (Restoration Comedy style drama based on *The Country Wife* by Wycherley –
> famously banned from print for almost 200 years and considered too
> outrageous to be performed at all.)

Wishing Well.
> (Restoration Comedy style drama based on *Epsom Wells* by the Poet Laureate,
> *Shadwell.* Long forgotten and out of print due to lewdness, this wonderful play
> had a fine balance of bawdiness with delicious satire and biting wit.)

Great Fairy Tales of the World. Vol. 1
> Dramatised in English for Encyclopaedia Britannica Japan.

Great Fairy Tales of the World. Vol. 2
> Dramatised in English for Encyclopaedia Britannica Japan.

The Star Crossed Lovers.
> (*Romeo and Juliet* faithfully translated line-by-line for modern audiences and
> education)

She Who Would Be King.
> (*Macbeth* faithfully translated line-by-line for modern audiences and education)

Love's Last Shift
> Mr Loveless has been away for ten years. Dividing his time between brothel
> and bottle he no longer recognizes his wife, Amanda, when he returns to
> London. Acting the part of a high-class lady of the night, Amanda entices Mr
> Loveless into her luxurious house and treats him to the night of his dreams,
> only confessing her true identity in the morning. Banished for lewdness for 300
> years.

For further titles and information visit www.century-17.com

CONTENTS

CAST LIST
in order of convenience

Mr Harry Horner A wit about town with a roving eye and a reputation. A man who views women as objects solely placed upon this earth to be used to his advantage.

Mr Frank Hancock A wit about town and a romantic. In contrast to Mr Horner, he views women as objects of love - especially the intended wife of another man.

Mr Dick Uppington A wit about town with a roving eye for wenches. He likes his women common and feisty.

Mr Jack Pinchwife Jealous gentleman who took a young country wife as he "couldn't keep a whore in town". Overly protective, believes she will be corrupted by town ways and stray.

Mrs Margery Pinchwife A very young and attractive country wife. Innocent in the ways of the town, but with a keen desire to learn and experience them.

Alithea Pinchwife Sister of Mr Pinchwife, intended of Count Sparkish. An honourable woman, often the only voice of reason. Marrying for position in society.

Count Sparkish (pronounced Sparkeesh) A naïve man of dubious title and wit. Marrying for financial gain. Oblivious to his own faults and the taunts of others around him.

Sir Jasper Gooding A knight of the realm and a trusting man who puts business before love. Looking for distractions to prevent his pretty wife straying.

Lady Gooding Pretty wife of Sir Jasper. She married for position and plays the honourable wife whilst secretly looking for excitement she doesn't find in marriage.

Dainty Gooding Sister of Sir Jasper. Fun and flighty.

Dr Cracker A surgeon and a man of medicine with no scruples when financial reward is offered.

Anita Quim A young lady of fine repute in an unfulfilled marriage, cousin of Lady Gooding

Old Lady Quim Grandmother of Anita Quim. Old fashioned, keeps an eye on her granddaughter's behaviour.

Lucy Maid and Attendant to Alithea Pinchwife. Willing to assist a man to her mistress's heart if her palm is crossed with silver.

Waiters, Servants and attendants as required.

Cuckold:
Noun, archaic: - the husband of an adulteress, often regarded as an object of derision.
Verb - to make a man a cuckold by having a sexual relationship with his wife.
In Plain language - A man whose wife is sleeping with another man or men.

TO TAKE A WIFE
An observation upon social consequences
by SJ Hills

ACT I

ACT I SCENE I. MR HORNER'S LODGINGS, LONDON TOWN

Russell Street

[MR HORNER IS PRESENT, ENTER DR CRACKER]

Horner / (excited) Well, my dear doctor, have you done as I requested?

Dr Cracker / Against my better judgement.

Horner / I'm not paying you to judge me. Have you told the townswomen my sad news?

Dr Cracker / Your reputation is undone forever with the women, Mr Horner. I have informed the whole town you are as useless as a eunuch with as much conviction as if I had made you one myself.

Horner / Have you told the old fumbling housekeepers this end of the town? They'll be keenest to spread the word.

Dr Cracker / I have told society women and their serving-women alike, and any women of the Exchange that would listen. Well, I say 'told' - I whispered it to them, so I've no doubt word will spread like wildfire, and by now you will be as desirable to the young women as...

Horner / ...as the pox. Good. I am only afraid it will not be believed. You told them I was in a French accident, and then ruined forever by a French surgeon?

Dr Cracker / Your recent journey to France has made it all the more credible, and your being here a fortnight before appearing in public looks to all purposes as if you were recuperating from your loss.

Horner / Excellent.

Dr Cracker / Well, I would be lying if I claimed never to have been hired by young gentlemen before to further their reputation among women, mostly with exaggerated tales, but you are the first who wished to be known as a man unfit for women.

Horner / My dear doctor, let vain rogues pretend to be abler men than they really are, as pretence is all they have to offer.

Dr Cracker / It's as ridiculous as us practitioners of medicine issuing notices renouncing our qualifications in the hope of gaining customers.

Horner / Ah, but you see, doctor, women are more concerned with preserving their reputations than for any wild boasts. A man who opens his mouth too readily is less likely to cause the same effect in a woman's legs.
And if cautious husbands are to be cheated of their wives, it will have to be with some new trick, so new it has never been tried before.

[KNOCK ON DOOR. ENTER SERVANT]

Servant / Sir Jasper Gooding and two women to see you, sir.

Horner / Damn! Sir Jasper, the stuffy old fool, and his women too.
-Show them in boy.
-They're probably here to see if the news on the street is true or not.

[EXIT SERVANT]

[ENTER SIR JASPER GOODING, LADY GOODING, AND MRS DAINTY GOODING]

Sir Jasper / Harry Horner, my dear fellow. My coach has just broken down outside your door, sir. I look upon this as a reprimand to me, sir, for not shaking your hand since your coming back from France, sir. And so my disaster, sir, has been my good fortune. And this is my wife and sister, sir.

Horner / (ignoring women) How are you, sir?

Sir Jasper / I am well, sir. And my lady, and sister, sir.
-Wife, this is Mr Horner.

Lady G / Thank you, husband. (offers her hand) Mr Horner.

Horner / Well, sir?

Sir Jasper / Won't you greet my lady wife with a kiss, sir?

Horner / I will kiss no man's wife, sir, for I have taken my eternal leave of the fairer sex, sir.

Sir Jasper / Would you not wish to be acquainted with my wife at least, sir?

Horner / She's a woman, sir, and consequently loathsome, sir. I loathe them almost as much as I do husbands.

Sir Jasper / You loathe husbands? Why, sir?

Horner / Because, sir, I can neither be one, and nor can I make a cuckold of one anymore, sir.

Sir Jasper / Ha! ha! ha! Mercury! Mercury! So the word on the street is true!

Lady G / Pray, Sir Jasper, let us be gone from this rude fellow.

Dainty / Who would think they let such common people into France these days?

Lady G / Foh! He's too much like a French fellow. They hate women of quality and virtue like us, and they detest women who marry for love as much as those who marry for money.

Dainty / Goodness. Who do they marry then?

Lady G / They marry an ugly brute for position and keep a pretty companion for company.

Horner / As the French say, 'Elles apparaîtrent tout la même par la derrière'.

Lady G / What did he say?

Dainty / (slowly trying to work out the literal meaning of Horner's schoolboy French)
All the girls... are the same... when... Oh!

Horner / (smugly) I thought you'd like it.

Lady G / When what?

Dainty / I am not sure I have it right. 'All the girls are the same when in the behind'? That doesn't make sense.

Horner / What? No, it says "they all look the same from behind", -but I preferred your version.

Lady G / Foh! Pray, let us be gone from this vulgar brute.

Horner / A wise decision, madam. For I have brought back nothing of interest to you, not a single bawdy picture, nor even a print of the updated sexual positions manual, -although just for you I did bring back a copy of 'Sex In The Convent'...

Dr Cracker / Shame on you, sir! What ever are you thinking? There are ladies present.

Sir Jasper / Ha! ha! ha! He definitely hates women, that's for sure.

Dainty / (ambiguous) Such a shame.

Lady G / Foh! He's such a rude, low fellow. The type that finds women who shamelessly flaunt their affections more desirable than those of us with honourable virtues.

Horner / Your virtue being your only desirable affection, madam.

Lady G / Why, you saucy fellow! You would seek to dishonour my reputation?

Horner / If I could, nothing would give me greater pleasure.

Lady G / Oh the filthy French beast! Foh! Why do we stay?

Sir Jasper / Ha! ha! ha! He can't damage your ladyship's reputation, upon my honour. Poor man.

Lady G / Let us be gone. I can endure his vile company no longer.

Sir Jasper / Wait until the driver comes with a fresh coach. It'll be here presently. I cannot stay, it's, let me see, a quarter and a half quarter of a minute past eleven. The council will be sitting. I must be away. Business must always come first before love and pleasure, Mr Horner. The words of the wise.

Horner / And the impotent, Sir Jasper.

Sir Jasper / Aye, aye, and the impotent, Mr Horner. hah! hah! hah!

Lady G / What, and leave us with this filthy minded man alone in his lodgings?

Sir Jasper / He's a harmless man now, you know. Wait here, I'll hasten the coach to you.
(bow of head, shake of hand) Mr Horner, your servant. I should be glad to see you at my house. Please, come dine with me and play games with my wife after dinner, as you are now suitable for a woman's after dinner pleasure, ha! ha!

Horner / Me? Suitable for a woman's pleasure, sir?

Sir Jasper / It is a husband's job to provide innocent diversion for a wife and who better to employ than your good self. Ha! Ha! Farewell.

Horner / Your servant, Sir Jasper. I shall endeavour to fulfil your desires – and your wife's.

[EXIT SIR JASPER]

Lady G / Foh! I will not stay.

Horner / Stay, I beseech you, madam, surely you must be curious to know if I can still offer the ladies what they truly desire?

Lady G / No, no, foh! You have nothing I desire.

Dainty / You can offer ladies what they desire?

Lady G / No, no, no, Dainty! foh! foh! foh! We are leaving. Come along.

[EXIT LADY GOODING USHERING OUT MRS DAINTY GOODING]

Dr Cracker / Now, you have completely ruined your reputation with the women I think.

Horner / You are an ass, doctor. Don't you see? Already, upon hearing my story and seeing my behaviour this upstanding gentleman, this knight of the realm, despite my previous reputation leaves his wife in my lodgings, and then invites me to his house later to play games with her. Already!

Dr Cracker / By this method you may win over the husbands, but not the wives.

Horner / You wait. If I can abuse their husbands trust, I'll soon be abusing their wives.

Dr Cracker / And your old dalliances?

Horner / Those boring insatiable wenches. I have my eye on bigger fish now, and the next best thing to making a new mistress is being rid of an old one.

Dr Cracker / But how will you get any new ones?

Horner / My dear doctor, any huntsman will tell you he spends more time seeking the game than he does running it down. Women of quality are so civil in their behaviour we cannot distinguish their intentions. How does one know who will or will not? A good sport is hard to spot, a man is easily mistaken. Now I can be sure.

Dr Cracker / I'm sure I don't understand how.

Horner / It's easy. The woman who shows a disliking towards me loves the sport - like those women who just left. I guarantee they are fair game.

Dr Cracker / Surely disliking you is the opposite effect you would wish.

Horner / Not at all. They only dislike me because I can not offer what they desire. Women of honour, as they call themselves, are only careful of their reputations, not their persons. It is scandal they wish to avoid, not men. My reputation as a eunuch allows me privileges no man could ever have. I can be seen in a lady's bedchamber with no damage to her honour, I can even kiss innocent young ladies in front of their loved ones. In short, it is my passport to every corner of the town. Well, doctor?

Dr Cracker / Perhaps you are the doctor now, offering relief to the needy. However your process is so new we do not know it will succeed.

Horner / Not so new the case is not already proven, doctor.

Dr Cracker / Well, I'll believe it only when I see it. I wish you luck, and many patients. But now, I have mine to attend to. Farewell.

[EXIT DR CRACKER]

ACT I SCENE II. A GENTLEMAN'S CLUB IN TOWN

[HORNER IS SITTING WITH A PAPER AND A
BOTTLE OF WINE]

[ENTER HANCOCK AND UPPINGTON WHO JOIN
HIM. A WAITER BRINGS WINE]

Hancock / Good day to you, Mr Horner. I am glad to see you in good spirits
after your ordeal facing the public yesterday. The contempt of the
women and the mockery of the men at the play could not have
been the easiest of things to endure.

Horner / Thank you, Mr Hancock. I did bear it bravely, didn't I?

Uppington / With a most theatrical impudence I thought, and with more
cockiness than the orange-selling wenches there, - though perhaps
not the wisest choice of words – certainly more dramatic than one
of those great pot-bellied actresses.

Horner / What about the ladies, Dick? What did they say? Did they have no
pity?

Hancock / Ladies? Stuck-up prigs, they'd never pity a fellow who'd lost
everything.

Horner / And the women in the boxes?

Uppington / Pah, they would never have lain with you even for pity - when it
was still in your power of course.

Hancock / Those women think it a pity every man who dallies with common
women isn't afflicted like you.

Horner / Well, a pox on them! Since I can't enjoy their company, I shall
enjoy yours all the more instead, gentlemen. (raises glass) Good
fellowship, and manly pleasures.

Hancock / (raises glass) And good feminine pleasures. They add relish to the
other.

Horner / Nay. They disturb one another.

Hancock / Poppycock! Not in moderation. Mistresses are like books. If you bury yourself in them they tire you and make you unfit for company. But if thumbed lightly, your company and conversation is so much the better for it.

Uppington / Yes, a mistress should be like a little country retreat. Not to dwell in constantly, only for the odd night away. The better to taste the town when a man returns.

Horner / Women's sole purpose is for man's advantage. When it comes to marriage, he that lives well and dines well, married well. He that lives poorly and dines poorly, married poorly. Money or love? You cannot have both. You have to sacrifice one for the other. So, which is it to be? Fine wine, or good love?

Hancock / Give me love every time!

Horner / Are you sure? Wine gives you liberty, love takes it from you.

Uppington / Gad, he's not wrong either.

Hancock / But love gives you joy, Horner.

Horner / No, wine gives you joy, love gives you grief and torture, - before the surgeon anyway.
Wine makes us witty, love makes a man dull and drives him to drink.
Love and wine, like oil and vinegar.

Hancock / I grant you it probably is, but love will still be uppermost in my mind.

Horner / Not for my part, I will have only those glorious manly pleasures of being very drunk and very slovenly.

Hancock / And very stupid.

Uppington / Which reminds me, Count Sparkish said he would meet us here after some business he had to tend to.

Hancock / What? My dear friend, Sparky? Though I sometimes think he is only fond of me because of my abuse of him.

Uppington / No, the opinion he holds of himself is so high he could not bring himself to believe people ridicule him.

Horner / Well, there's another pleasure drinking brings about I didn't think of - I shall lose his acquaintance because he cannot drink. And you know how very hard it is to be rid of him, and his nauseous pretence of wit.

Hancock / A man who only by being in the company of men of wit could pass for one.

Horner / Only to the short-sighted world. His company is as troublesome as a cuckold whose wife you have a mind to take.

Hancock / And he spoils our enjoyment by constantly raping our conversation.

Horner / And in trying to pass for a wit about town, shows himself up as a fool every night.

Uppington / Though in fairness, gentlemen, we are secretly guilty of helping in his downfall.

Hancock/ Perhaps, but though snubbed, embarrassed, and abused, the rogue still hangs on.

Horner / A pox on all the pretenders who act out a pretence yet still appear exactly as nature intended.

Uppington / Most men are contrary to how they seem though. Your bully is just a coward with a weapon in his hand, and your rich upstanding money lender? In reality nothing but a poor rogue who never spends a penny more than is wrung out of him.

Hancock / Aye, the likes of us, laying out daily on new purchases of pleasure, we are the truly wealthy ones.

Uppington / Aye, the ladies in Madame Lantalu's say they have the hardest job in the world emptying the sacks of the money men, whereas our deposits are by far the more generous and easier to collect.

Horner / And the man who most jealously guards his wife – he'll be the man with the cheating wife...

> [HORNER SPIES SPARKISH ENTERING THE DOOR AT THIS POINT. HE CONTINUES TALKING AS SPARKISH SPOTS THE GROUP AND HEADS FOR THEM]

Horner / ...and the noisy impudent rogue of a wit who thinks his conversation sparkling? – the greatest show-off, dullest ass, and the worst possible company... as you shall see, for here he comes now.

Sparkish / How goes it, Horner? How's things?

Horner / Sparky, we were just talking about you.

Sparkish / It's SparkEESH. Count Sparkish. Anyway, I have heard the talk in town about you too, Harry, ha! ha! ha! I am sure Dick and Frank would like to hear it, shall I tell you?

Horner / I am sure you will anyway, and be frightfully tedious.

Sparkish / Now then, since you are so brisk, and provoke me, you can take what follows. If you must know, I was talking and meeting with some ladies yesterday, and they happened to mention the fine new signs in town.

Horner / Very 'fine' ladies, I'm sure.

Sparkish / I said, I know where the best new sign is. Where? says one of the ladies. In Covent Garden, I replied. Another asked, In what street? In Russell Street, I replied. Lord, said another, I'm sure there was no new sign there yesterday. Oh, but there was, I said again, and it came out of France and has been there a fortnight.

Uppington / A pox on you! Enough of this drivel.

Horner / No, hear him out. Let him play his audience a while. It's not often he gets the opportunity.

Hancock / The worst speaker, yet the longest build up.

Sparkish / Not at all, It will make you laugh. It cannot be, says a third lady. Yes, yes, I said again. A fourth lady said…

Horner / How many more ladies?

Sparkish / No, no more. Listen. I said to the fourth, Did you never see Mr Horner? He lodges in Russell Street, and he's a good sign of a man, you know, since he came out of France. ha! ha! ha!

Horner / The devil take me. Yours is the sign of an idiot.

Sparkish / With that they all fell about laughing till they pissed themselves. What? it does not move you? My wit is obviously too good for you, and a jest without laughter is like a huntsman without a horn, eh Horner? Ha! Ha! Ha!
     (no one else laughs) Come, come, Horner, where should we dine? I have left an earl at Whitehall to dine with you.

Uppington / But I thought you preferred the company of a title better than us mere wits, Sparky.

Hancock / Best go back to him.

Sparkish / No, sir. To me, a witty intellect is the greatest title in the world.

Horner / Go dine with your earl, sir. We are your friends, we will not think it poor form if you left, I assure you.

Hancock / Indeed, you should go to him.

Sparkish / No, I beg you, gentlemen.

Uppington / We'll throw you out if you don't. We'll not have you disappoint someone for our sake.

[THEY TAKE HIS ARM TO USHER HIM OUT]

Sparkish / No, dear gentlemen, hear me out.

Horner / No, no, sir, not by any means. Now go, sir.

[THEY USHER HIM TO THE DOOR FORCIBLY]

Sparkish / Why, my dear rogues…

Uppington / No, no. Out!

[THEY ALL THRUST HIM OUT OF THE DOOR,
SLAMMING IT AFTER HIM]

All / Ha! ha! ha!

[THE DOOR RE-OPENS AND SPARKISH POPS HIS
HEAD BACK IN]

Sparkish / But, Horner, please hear me out. I find wit as necessary at dinner
as a glass of good wine. That's why I never have any stomach
when I eat alone. Come, where shall we dine?

Horner / Wherever you say.

Sparkish / At Lanterlu's?

Uppington / Yes, if you like.

Sparkish / Or the Cock?

Uppington / Yes, I hear you like the Cock.

Sparkish / Or the Dog and Partridge then?

Horner / Aye, if you have a mind to it.   We shan't be dining at any of
them.

[A CLOCK CHIMES IN THE DISTANCE]

Sparkish / Pish! Look at the time. With your fooling around we shall miss the
new play, and I would not miss the opening performance any more
than I would miss sitting in the intellect's row. I must fetch my
mistress and be away.

[EXIT COUNT SPARKISH. THEY ALL SIT DOWN
AGAIN LAUGHING]
[MR PINCHWIFE ARRIVES AT THE DOOR AND
ENTERS]

Horner / Grief! Who have we here now? (by way of greeting) Mr Pinchwife, sir, join us.

Mr Pinch / Gentlemen.

Horner / Well, Jack, from your long absence out of town, the grimness of your manner and the slovenliness of your attire, I should be giving you congratulations, should I not?

Mr Pinch / Congratulations?

Horner / For your marriage?

Mr Pinch / God's truth! Marriage? No, no, no. My long stay in the country will excuse my dress, and I have a lawsuit that brings me to town which takes the humour from me. Besides, I was hoping to catch Count Sparkish here, I must give him five thousand pounds tomorrow to marry my sister.

Horner / You country gentlemen will buy anything it seems. And his is a crooked title, if we want to quibble about it. Well, am I to give congratulations? I heard you were married.

Mr Pinch / And you believe everything you hear?

Horner / I must confess, I did not expect marriage from such an old whoremaster as you. One that frequented the town night life and knew the women so well.

Mr Pinch / Nay, I have married no wife in town.

Horner / Pshaw! It's all the same. You take the 'safe' option of marrying a country wife rather than a pampered, Piccadilly hussy, - and then find you've been cheated by a chum in the country while you were in town.

Mr Pinch / A pox on that! Our country wives are not like your town women, sir.

Uppington / So he did marry a country wife after all, the sly old goat.

Mr Pinch / At least we are surer of the breed there, know what her keeping has been, whether spoiled or soiled.

Horner / Come, come, to my certain knowledge there has been a case of the clap as far away as Wales, and I have heard tales of countrymen going to family reunions solely to meet women. -So, is she young and pretty?

Mr Pinch / No, no, no. She is no beauty, her only attraction is her youth and modesty. Wholesome, homely, and housewifely, that's all.

Uppington / He sounds like a pig farmer the way he describes her.

Mr Pinch / She's too awkward, ill-mannered, and silly to bring to town.

Hancock / Then I think you should bring her, to be taught good breeding.

Mr Pinch / To be taught! No thank you, sir. Good wives should be kept ignorant. I'll keep her from your advice, be sure of it.

Hancock / I do believe the rogue is jealous, as if his wife were not ignorant.

Horner / If she is unattractive, there will be less danger here than leaving her in the country. We have such a variety of dainties in town we are seldom hungry.

Uppington / And they have coarse, hungry stomachs in the country.

Hancock / Nothing with a pulse is safe.

Uppington / And the hospitality is renowned there.

Hancock / Open house, every man welcome.

Mr Pinch / So, so, gentlemen.

Horner / But tell me, why did you marry her if she is so ugly, ill-bred, and silly? She must be stinking rich.

Mr Pinch / Worth twenty thousand of your town pounds, and you can be sure she'll not spend her portion. You can't say the same for your London baggage.

Horner / So you married a silly, ugly wife for her money. A lifetime of torture for a purse of gold.

Mr Pinch / Well, since she's ugly she's likelier to stay mine, and more importantly, being silly and innocent she does not know the difference between a man of twenty-one and one of forty.

Horner / Nine, if memory serves me right. And if she is so silly and innocent, surely she'll expect as much from a man of forty-nine as one of twenty-one.

Mr Pinch / Pshaw! I can do for her as two twenty-one year olds could, stamina is my middle name.

Horner / Really? I imagine the priest who married you was surprised. And what of her mind? Do country girls have good, 'creative' minds?

Mr Pinch / Oh no, sir, my wife has no mind of her own. She does as she is told, whether she agrees to it or not.

Horner / What a pity, I think a young woman is never ugly if she has a good mind.

Mr Pinch / What good would that be? Except in helping her fool around and making a fool of her husband.

Horner / Good for keeping it from his knowledge.

Mr Pinch / A fool cannot contrive to make her husband a cuckold.

Horner / Perhaps, but she'll entertain a man who can.

Mr Pinch / Well, I for one shall take care my wife does not cuckold me, even with your help, Mr Horner. I understand the ways of the town, sir.

Uppington / Ha! Ha! His help!

Hancock / He's newly arrived in town it seems, and has not heard how things are with him.

Horner / But tell me, Pinchwife, has marriage cured you from whoring? I hear it seldom does.

Hancock / 'Tis more than he can manage at his age.

Horner / The marriage vow is like the gambler's oath. A man limits himself to a small sum to play with, but this just makes him eager for more.

Uppington / Aye, aye, a man will be a gambler whilst his money holds out, a whoremaster whilst his vigour holds out, and a husband until he is found out.

Mr Pinch / Well, gentlemen, you may scorn me, but you will never know my wife. I know this town.

Horner / But tell me, was the way you were before not better? Isn't keeping a mistress better than marriage?

Mr Pinch / A pox on it! The hussies would cheat on me, I could never keep a whore to myself.

Horner / So, there we have it. You only married to keep a whore to yourself. Very well, but let me tell you, women are made loyal by good pay rather than vows of allegiance. I advise my friends to keep a woman or two rather than marry one, and anyway, as I saw by your example yesterday, your theory does not hold true.

Mr Pinch / What do you mean?

Horner / I saw you yesterday in the eight-penny seats with a pretty, young wench.

Mr Pinch / How the devil! I sat there so that she might not be seen. She'll never go to a play again.

Horner / What! Do you blush? At forty-nine? For having been seen with a wench?

Uppington / No, I warrant it was his wife he seated there out of sight. As he told us, he's a cunning old rogue and understands the ways of the town.

Hancock / He blushes again. Then it was his wife! Ha! Ha! Men these days are more ashamed to be seen with their wives in public than a wench.

Mr Pinch / Hell and damnation!

Horner / Was it your wife? She was exceedingly pretty. I was in love with her even at that distance.

Mr Pinch / And that is the closest you will be getting to her.
(preparing to leave) Your servant, gentlemen

Horner / No, stay I say.

Mr Pinch / I cannot, and will not.

Horner / Come, you shall dine with us.

Mr Pinch / I have dined already.

Horner / Come, I know you have not. I'll treat you, my dear rogue. You'll spend none of your Hampshire money today.

Mr Pinch / Treat me? You speak to me as if I were your cuckold already.

Horner / Not at all, I enjoy your company.

Mr Pinch / I must go, I have business at home. [gruffly] Good day, sirs.

[EXIT PINCHWIFE]

Hancock / Gone to beat his wife no doubt. He's as jealous as a Cheapside husband with a Convent Garden wife.

Horner / An old whoremaster who turns his back on wenching will always be jealous – those that escaped the pox that is. He knows the score too well, and jealousy is by far the worst disease of love.

End of Act I

ACT II

ACT II SCENE I. MR PINCHWIFE'S LODGINGS

[MRS MARGERY PINCHWIFE AND HER SISTER-IN-LAW ALITHEA PINCHWIFE ARE PRESENT]

Mrs Pinch / Pray, sister, where are the best green spaces to walk in London?

Alithea / Walk, Margery? Why, Mulberry Garden and St. James's Park. Or for a closer walk, the New Exchange.

Mrs Pinch / Alithea, tell me, why is my husband so glum here in town? He will not let me go out walking, and he would not let me wear my best gown yesterday.

Alithea / Oh, he is jealous, Margery.

Mrs Pinch / Jealous? Why?

Alithea / He's afraid you would love another man.

Mrs Pinch / Why should he be afraid of me loving another man when he will not let me talk to any other men!

Alithea / Did he not take you to a play yesterday?

Mrs Pinch / Aye, but we sat amongst ugly people. He would not let me near the gentry.

Alithea / Did you not see the fine gentlemen?

Mrs Pinch / They were sat under us where I could not see them. He told me only the naughty women sat there, and that they ruffle and tousle with the gentlemen and sometimes even sit on their laps! But even so, I would have ventured there.

Alithea / But how did you like the play?

Mrs Pinch / The play wearied me, Alithea, but I liked the actors enormously. They were good, proper men, sister!

Alithea / Oh, but you must not like the actors, Margery.

Mrs Pinch / But, how can I help it? -Tell me, sister, when my husband comes in, will you ask permission for me to go out walking?

Alithea / Out walking? Lord, does a country wife require airing like her husband's horses?

Mrs Pinch / Please, Alithea.

Alithea / All right. When your husband comes home I'll ask him, though I'm sure he'll not allow it.

Mrs Pinch / He says I can't go out for fear of catching the pox.

Alithea / Fy! Small-pox you should say, the other means something else.

[ENTER MR PINCHWIFE]

Mrs Pinch / Oh, my dear, dear husband, welcome home! Why do you look so angry? Has someone upset you?

Mr Pinch / You're a fool, wife!

[MRS PINCHWIFE BURSTS INTO TEARS]

Alithea / Goodness, so she is, crying for no reason, silly creature!

Mr Pinch / What? You would rather she was an impudent, wayward flirt like yourself? A cheap, notorious towns-woman?

Alithea / Brother, you are my only critic, and the honour of your family will suffer sooner through your wife than through me, even though I have the innocent liberty of the town.

Mr Pinch / Do not talk that way in front of my wife. - The innocent liberty of the town indeed!

Alithea / Then tell me, who boasts of any intrigue with me? I do not keep company with any women of scandalous reputation.

Mr Pinch / No, you keep company with men of scandalous reputation.

Alithea / Where have you ever seen me with a man that was not civil and proper? In a box at the theatre? In a drawing-room in Whitehall? In St. James's Park, or...

Mr Pinch / Do not teach my wife where the men are to be found! I believe she's the worse for you telling her the ways of the town already. Keep her in ignorance, as I do.

Mrs Pinch / (sniffing back the tears) Don't be angry with her, husband, she tells me nothing of the town, though I ask her a thousand times a day.

Mr Pinch / You are very inquisitive to know, I see?

Mrs Pinch / No indeed, dear. I hate London. Our place in the country is worth a thousand of it. I want to go back there again!

Mr Pinch / So you shall, soon enough. But weren't you talking of plays and players when I came in?
[to Alithea] You are the one who encourages her in such discourses, Alithea.

Mrs Pinch / No, indeed she is not, dear, she chided me just now for liking the actor men.

Mr Pinch / Liking the actor men! Mind you, if you can confess to liking them so openly you can't think them better than me, I suppose.

Mrs Pinch / But indeed, I do think them better than you.

Mr Pinch / What!

Mrs Pinch / At acting, dearest.

Mr Pinch / But you don't 'like' them better than me I hope.

Mrs Pinch / You are my own dear husband, and I know you. You know how I hate strangers, and strange things.

Mr Pinch / Strange things?

Mrs Pinch / The strange things you like, dearest.

Mr Pinch / They are the things a good wife does with her husband, not like the naughty townswomen who hate their husbands and do them with every other man.

Mrs Pinch / What else do townswomen do, dearest?

Mr Pinch / They like gossiping, drinking, fussy food, expensive clothes, and worst of all, spending their husband's money.

Mrs Pinch / Well, if to enjoy all these things is town-life, London is not such a bad place, dear.

Mr Pinch / What? No wife of mine will ever enjoy what London has to offer.

Alithea / So, you forbid me from showing her the pleasures of the town, and then go filling her head with the wonder of them yourself.

Mrs Pinch / But tell me, husband, why have we no actor-men in the country?

Mr Pinch / Ha! They don't understand men who wear tights in the country. Now don't ask me to go to a play again, Mrs Minx!

Mrs Pinch / But why, love? When you forbid me, you make me desire it all the more.

Alithea / Aye, forbidden fruit is always sweeter. (low) As I'm sure you'll discover soon enough.

Mrs Pinch / Please let me go to a play, dear.

Mr Pinch / Hold your peace, I will not.

Mrs Pinch / Why, love?

Mr Pinch / Why? I'll tell you why.

Alithea / (aloud to self) And give her even more reason to desire it.

Mr Pinch / First, you seem to like the gentlemen there, and second, they may like you.

Mrs Pinch / What, a homely country girl? No, dear, nobody will like me.

Mr Pinch / I'm telling you, they will.

Mrs Pinch / No, no. I know you are teasing me.

Mr Pinch / Teasing? I will tell you then, one of the lewdest fellows in town saw you there and told me he was in love with you.

Mrs Pinch / Indeed? Who? Which fellow?

Mr Pinch / I have said too much already. Even now, I can see how overjoyed you are!

Mrs Pinch / No, no! You must tell me. Was it a Hampshire gentleman? One of our neighbours? I promise you, I must give my proper thanks to him.

Mr Pinch / I promise you, you won't, he would ruin you, as he has done hundreds before. His only love for women is to look upon them as objects and ruin them.

Mrs Pinch / But if he loves me, why would he want to ruin me? Answer me that. I think he would not. I know I would do him no harm.

Alithea / Ha! ha! ha!

Mr Pinch / That may very well be so, but I'll keep him from doing you any harm, or me either.

[DOOR BELL RINGS IN THE DISTANCE]

Mr Pinch / But here comes company, go to your room. Go on.

Mrs Pinch / But, tell me, husband, is the gentleman that loves me handsome?

Mr Pinch / Go on, baggage, go.

[THRUSTS HER THROUGH THE DOOR,
FOLLOWING AFTER HER, PUSHES THE DOOR TO
BEHIND HIM LEAVING IT AJAR, SPYING FROM
THE OTHER SIDE]
[ENTER SPARKISH AND HANCOCK]

Mr Pinch / (aside) What? Are all the lewd libertines of the town brought to
my lodging by this footloose, conceited man!

Sparkish / Here she is, Hancock. Well, do you approve my choice?-
(to Alithea) My dear little imp, Alithea, I told you I would
acquaint you with all my friends; the intelligentsia and the wits.

Mr Pinch / (aside, bitter, sarcastic) Aye, and they'll know her as well as you
will, I'll warrant.

Hancock / (kissing her hand obviously smitten) Madam, your company is
truly a pleasure.

Sparkish / This man, my pretty imp, is one of our friends who will dance in
celebration at our wedding tomorrow, and one you must always
make welcome with open arms.

Mr Pinch / (aside) Monstrous!

Sparkish / Well, Hancock, how do you like her, eh? -My dear, do not avert
your eyes. I should hate a wife of mine to feel uncomfortable if I
show off her beauty to my friends.

Mr Pinch / (aside sarcastic) How caring of you!

Sparkish / Well, Hancock? What do you think?

Hancock / (smitten – still holding her hand from the kiss) I now wish I had a
mistress exactly like her in every way, except for her love for
you.

Alithea / (pulling her hand away) The Count has often told me his
acquaintances were all wits and jokers, now I find it to be true.

Sparkish / No, by the universe, madam, he is not joking, I assure you. He is
the most honest, worthy, true-hearted gentleman to a lady.

Mr Pinch / (aside) Praising another man to his mistress now!

Hancock / Sir, you flatter me, beyond expectation…

Sparkish / Not at all, I can see in your eyes you admire her.
          -He does admire you, madam.
          -You do don't you, Hancock?

Hancock / (mesmerised by her beauty) Such female beauty. Till now I never
          thought I would be envying you, or any man about to marry, but
          you have the best excuse for marriage I ever saw.

Alithea / Now I am satisfied you are one of the wits and jokers, sir.

Hancock / How so?

Alithea / Your being an enemy of marriage. I hear you wits hate it as
          much as work or bad wine.

Hancock / Truly, madam, I was never an enemy of marriage until now.

Alithea / But why is marriage an enemy to you now? Because it robs you
          of your friend here? Do you look upon a married friend, as one
          gone into a monastery?

Hancock / I do indeed, and it is because 'you' are marrying him. I trust,
          madam, you understand my meaning. I confess, if it were in my
          power to break the match, by Heavens I would.

Sparkish / Poor Frank!

Alithea / Would you wish to be so unkind to me, sir?

Hancock / No, no, it is not because I wish to be unkind to you.

Sparkish / Poor Frank! No, it is only his kindness to me.

Mr Pinch / (aside) Great kindness to you indeed! Insensible fop, letting a
          man make love to your wife in front of your face!

Sparkish / Come, dear Frank, I know us men of wit often grieve for our deceased brothers in marriage like we do for those that died of the clap, but I say before my mistress here - upon my honour, you shall still enjoy my company.
-Isn't that right, Alithea?
-Come on, Frank, don't grieve for me.

Hancock / No, I assure you, I'll not grieve for 'you'.

Sparkish / Tell me, Frank, do you not think my wife here a fine person?

Alithea / (correcting him) Wife to be.

Hancock / So fine I would marry her tomorrow myself, just to gaze upon her beauty.

Sparkish / But by the world, she has wit as well as beauty. Go with her into a corner, and see for yourself. Talk to her about anything, she is bashful in front of me.

Hancock / (offering his arm) Then, madam, come, let us see if you can be more open in a corner.

Alithea / Sir? You dispose of me before I had the pleasure of your time!

Sparkish / Nay, nay, madam, let me have a sign of your obedience, or... just go, madam!

                    [HANCOCK COURTS ALITHEA ASIDE]
                    [MR PINCHWIFE STEPS INTO THE ROOM FROM
                    HIS OBSERVATION POINT JUST OUTSIDE]

Mr Pinch / Why, sir! If you are not concerned for the honour of your wife, I am for that of my sister. I will not let you debauch her. A pimp to your own wife! Bringing men to her and letting them make love before your face? Thrusting them into a corner together? Is this your town wit and conduct?

Sparkish / Ha! ha! ha! A smart-arse brother, eh?. Something I find more laughable than a downright fool, ha! ha! I shall burst with mirth. Nay, you will not disturb them. By the world, I'll make you sorry if you try. – Now leave.

[SPARKISH ESCORTS PINCHWIFE FORCIBLY OUT OF THE ROOM AND THE ARGUMENT CONTINUES IN THE NEXT ROOM INDISTINCT TO THE AUDIENCE UNDER THE FOLLOWING CONVERSATION BETWEEN HANCOCK AND ALITHEA]

Hancock / So, dearest madam, is there nothing I could do to dissuade you from marrying tomorrow?

Alithea / The bands are read, the license drawn up, arrangements made. Nothing would dissuade me now.

Hancock / Not even if I proclaimed my undying love for you?

Alithea / I had his before.

Hancock / You never had it. Can't you see, he lacks jealousy, the only infallible sign of it.

Alithea / Because I have given him no reason to doubt my virtue. Besides, he loves me, or he would not marry me.

Hancock / Marrying you tomorrow is as much a sign of his love as bribing your maid is a sign of his generosity.

Alithea / What are you saying, sir?

Hancock / Shall we say, he was protecting his interests.

Alithea / And what better way to protect his interests than by marriage?

Hancock / Unless he is marrying for interest rather than love. He that marries into a fortune covets the mistress for her money, not her love. If you want marriage as a sign of love, take it from me right here, right now.

Alithea / I cannot, though now you have put a doubt in my head. But I must marry him, my reputation in society would suffer otherwise.

Hancock / No. Begging your pardon, madam, but your reputation in society would suffer 'by' marrying him.

Alithea / Well, now you are being rude, sir.
(calls loudly) Count Sparkish, pray come here, your friend here is
being very troublesome, and very forward with his love.

Hancock / (to Alithea) No! No, wait!

Mr Pinch / (off loudly) Did you hear that, eh?

Sparkish / (off loudly) Why? Do you think I should be jealous like a country
bumpkin?

Mr Pinch / (off loudly) No, like a cuckold, like a gullible towns-person
count.

Sparkish / (off loudly) Like a gullible, country, pie-eating, pig-poking,
buffoon like you!
You will stay here, I can trust my wife in another man's hands.
Where do you keep yours, eh? Locked up in the sty with the other
piggies? Oink Oink!

Mr Pinch / (off struggling) I am warning you, sir. I am not a man to trifle
with.

[SOUNDS OF A STRUGGLE ARE HEARD WITHIN]

Hancock / Madam, you could have been a little less generous in telling him.

Alithea / And you could have been a little less generous in wronging him.

Hancock / Wronging him! No man could wrong him, nature has beaten us to
it. He is far too dense to damage. Full of hot air, a coward, a
senseless idiot, a wretch so contemptible to all the world but you,
that…

Alithea / (slaps his face – but not so hard that it is real anger)
Do not rail against him, sir, he is to be my husband, therefore I
am resolved to like him. More over, I am obliged to tell him you
are not his friend.
(calls) Count Sparkish. Count Sparkish!

[PINCHWIFE AND SPARKISH RETURN
HURRIEDLY TO THE ROOM]

Sparkish / What, what?-
(to Hancock) Now, dear rogue, does she not have wit?

Hancock / (surly, and rubbing side of face) Not as much as I thought, and hoped she had.

Alithea / Count Sparkish, do you bring people to rail against you?

Hancock / (in protest) Madam I...

Sparkish / If he does rail against me, it is done in jest, I'll warrant. It's what we wits do for one another, do not take any notice of it.

Alithea / He spoke so scurrilously of you, I had no patience to hear him out. Besides, he attempted to make love with me.

Sparkish / Pshaw! To show his intellect. - We wits tease and flirt openly, but only to show our intellect. We have no affections so we have no malice.

Alithea / He said you were a contemptible person, too dense to damage

Sparkish / Pshaw!

Alithea / Full of hot air...

Sparkish / Pshaw!

Alithea / A coward...

Sparkish / Pshaw, pshaw!

Alithea / A senseless, drivelling idiot...

Sparkish / What! Does he ridicule my intellect? I can't allow that, by the world.
- Brother Pinchwife, help me kill him, since I have just cause -
and the odds are on my side.
-Draw, sir!

Alithea / Wait! Stop!

Sparkish What, what?

Alithea / (flattered by Sparkish defending her honour, and also of
Hancock's attention)
I can not let you kill the gentleman. Because of his kindness to
me I am far from hating him, and if my honour was ever at stake
with the gentleman…

Sparkish / …it will be the death of him!

Alithea / Wait, wait! Indeed, to tell the truth, the gentleman also said, that
what he spoke was out of friendship for you.

Sparkish / What! What are you saying? I am a fool? Then I am not a fool?
A 'drivelling idiot' but said out of friendship to me?

Alithea / Yes, to see whether I was concerned enough for you. He made
love to me only to be satisfied of my virtue, for your sake.

Hancock / Done in kindness, however.

Sparkish / Well, if that is so, my dear rogue, I beg your pardon. But why did
you not you tell me so? Honestly!

Hancock / Because I did not think it important, honestly.

Sparkish / Come on, let's go to the new play. Horner is not here, and I'm not
missing it. He'll have to meet us there. Come, madam.

Alithea / I will not go if you intend to leave me alone in my box and run
into the pit, as you usually do.

Sparkish / Pshaw! I'll leave Hancock to entertain you in your box, that's just
as good. If I stayed with you I would be thought no judge of the
action. Come on, Hancock, escort her down.

[EXEUNT SPARKISH, HANCOCK, AND ALITHEA]

Mr Pinch / (aside) Well, be on your way, idiotic king of the town fops.
You'll be a cuckold before you're even married. But now, I must
look after my own freehold.

ACT II SCENE II.   A LITTLE LATER IN MR PINCHWIFE'S LODGINGS

[MR PINCHWIFE IS AT A DESK WRITING AND BLOTTING HIS WORK. LADY GOODING, MRS DAINTY GOODING, AND ANITA QUIM ARRIVE]

Mr Pinch / (hearing the commotion) What the devil? What now!

Lady G / (entering the room) Good afternoon, sir. Where, pray, is your good lady, Mr Pinchwife? We've come to escort her to the new play.

Mr Pinch / New play?

Lady G / And my husband will call upon you presently.

Mr Pinch / Husband? Lady Gooding, I will not be seeing Sir Jasper till I have called upon him at his home. Nor shall my wife be seeing your ladyship till she has sent word she is to be expected.

Lady G / Not while we are here, sir?

Mr Pinch / No, Madam.

Dainty / Please, Mr Pinchwife, let us see her.

Anita Quim / Yes. We will not stir from here till we see her.

Mr Pinch / (under breath) A pox on you all!
(Goes to the door, checks it, and returns) She has locked the door, and she's gone out.

Lady G / No, you have locked the door, and she's in.

Dainty / They told us below she was here.

Mr Pinch / Well, (pause) to tell you the truth, ladies - which I was afraid to let you know before lest it might endanger your lives - my wife has just had the small-pox come out on her.
Do not be alarmed, but, you should not stay here and endanger your lives. I beg you, ladies, be gone while you still can.

Lady G / No, no, we have all had them.

Anita Quim / Regrettably!

Dainty / Come, come, we must see how she is. I understand the disease.

Lady G / Come along, Pinchwife!

Mr Pinch / (defeated aside) Damned, women. Such experts at the art of deception, they see right through me. Well if they will not leave...
(aloud) Oh! I just remembered I have to get her some medicine. Your servant, ladies.

[EXIT PINCHWIFE POST-HASTE LEAVING THE WOMEN STANDING THERE]

Anita Quim / Well, well. There's a fine example of jealousy!

Lady G / Indeed, most unusual, since wives are normally so neglected by their husbands.

Dainty / That's the truth! It's the wives who should be jealous.

Anita Quim / Yes indeed. These days men of quality spend all their energy and fortunes in chasing cheap little playhouse creatures, foh!

Dainty / Leaving us women of quality neglected, for the sake of a tuppenny trollop, foh!

Lady G / She speaks the truth. It's an utter shame us women of quality should be so slighted. I think breeding should stand for something. Why, just last week I saw a man with a title chasing a cheap harlot for a kiss in the gentlemen's area.

Dainty / Aye, it is not right men of honour should love below their ranks, any more than they should marry.

Lady G / Fy, fy, upon them! They now seem to think cross breeding is as good for themselves as it is for their dogs and horses.

Dainty / And, telling all kinds of things about us in their stories, telling all the world they have lain with us.

Lady G / Damned rascals! To tell another man he has had a person when he has not had a person is the greatest wrong in the whole world that can be done to a person.

Dainty / Would it be forgivable if they 'had' lain with us and boasted of it?

Lady G / Sister! Think of what are you saying!

Anita Quim / 'Tis a shame to our honour that we should be so wronged.

Lady G / 'Tis a greater shame to our honour to be found associating with such lowly men, foh!

Dainty / Isn't the crime against our honour the same with a man of quality as with any other?

Lady G / Certainly not! The man of quality is most like one's husband, and therefore the fault would be less.

Dainty / But then, of course, the pleasure would be less.

Lady G / Fy, fy, fy, for shame, sister! Where is this conversation going? Be cautious in your discourse, or I shall hate you.

Dainty / Besides, an affair is so much more scandalous the greater the man's quality. And exciting – I shouldn't wonder.

Anita Quim / But nobody takes notice of an ordinary man, and therefore with him it is easier to keep secret. And there is no crime if nobody knows.

Lady G / Indeed, I do think you are right. A husband's reputation remains intact as long as our honour remains intact. So a woman of honour must chose wisely in order to retain her dear honour.

Dainty / (cheekily) So, which fellow did you chose wisely, sister?

Lady G / I still have my dear, dear honour, dear.
Come, let us go to the Exchange, we'll be late for the play.

ACT II SCENE III. THE NEW EXCHANGE

The New Exchange, designed by Inigo Jones, was situated on the Strand near Covent Garden.
A shopping district outside the City walls with a specialized selection of goods for sale.
Shopping fulfilled an important social function; places to meet people and fashion centres to be seen at, many individual shops also serving as casual social clubs.

[LADY GOODING, DAINTY AND ANITA ARE PRESENT.
ENTER SIR JASPER GOODING, HORNER, AND UPPINGTON]

Sir Jasper / Ah, my dear honourable wife. I apologise for keeping you waiting, I had some business to discuss with these gentlemen.

Horner / (bowing) Ladies, I am honoured.

Lady G / What do you mean by bringing these uncouth men to us, husband?

Dainty / Foh! These men are as bad as wits.

Anita Quim / Foh!

Lady G / Ladies, let us leave.

Sir Jasper / Stay, stay. Indeed, to tell you the naked truth-

Lady G / Fy, Sir Jasper! Do not use that word, 'naked', in front of ladies.

Sir Jasper / Very well, dear. In short I have business at Whitehall, and cannot go to the play with you, therefore you will have to go without me.

Lady G / To the play with those two?

Sir Jasper / No, no, with Mr Horner, not the other. There is no more scandal being seen with him than with old Mr Tattler.

Lady G / With that nasty fellow! No-no.

Sir Jasper / Now, come, come dear. You know I have business to attend to, I would accompany you if I could, and he is harmless now.

Horner / Ladies, while they argue...

[HORNER AND UPPINGTON DRAW NEAR ANITA QUIM AND DAINTY GOODING]

Dainty / Stand away, Horner. You are one of the wits, you are obscenity through and through.

Anita Quim / Yes, stand away, sirs, you make us nauseous.

Uppington / Who the devil are these women, Horner?

Horner / My dear, Uppinton, these are women who like to make a great pretence of honour by criticising and sneering at ladies of quality, in the same way the dull critics sneer at men of intellect, in the knowledge they will never be one.

Sir Jasper / Come, Mr Horner, I must insist you go with these ladies to the play, sir.

Horner / I, sir?

Sir Jasper / Yes you, sir. Hurry, hurry.

Horner / I must beg your pardon, sir, and theirs, but I will not be seen in a woman's company in public again for all the world.

Anita Quim / No, he wants a woman's company in private.

Sir Jasper / The poor man! Not him! ha! ha! Have you not heard the news, Mrs Quim?

Dainty / These days it seems, lewd fellows feel greater shame being seen in a virtuous women's company, than virtuous women feel being seen with them.

Horner / Indeed, madam, there was a time when I hated virtuous women.

Anita Quim / And now?

Horner / Now I hate all women.

Lady G / And that would make you very good company, sir, for we would not be troubled by you.

Sir Jasper / Good, that is settled. In sober sadness, he shall go with you.

Uppington / If he will not, I am ready to escort the ladies, and I think I am the fitter man for the task.

Sir Jasper / You, sir? No, no, no. I thank you but no thank you. Master Horner is a privileged man now among the virtuous ladies. It'll be a great while before you are. he! he! he!
No, as I see it, the virtuous ladies have no business with you, Dick Uppington.

Uppington / It's strange how a man cannot be seen with virtuous women nowadays, unless he is fully equipped to enter the Great Turk's harem! Or perhaps under-equipped would be more accurate. - But talking of under-equipped, where is Pinchwife?

Lady G / I saw Mr Pinchwife scurrying towards his home just a short while ago, sir. Perhaps if you hurry you can catch him.

Uppington / Then if you'll forgive me ladies, I shall see you anon. Gentlemen.

[UPPINGTON NODS TO ALL AND LEAVES AT
SPEED]

Horner / Oh for an evening spent in the delights of the company of fine
minded gentlemen.

Sir Jasper / Come, come, Horner, what? Are you now completely avoiding
that soft, sweet, gentle, noble creature made for man's
companionship and pleasure?

Horner / Not at all, Sir Jasper. I enjoy the company of the noble spaniel.

Sir Jasper / Ha, Ha! I was referring to womankind.

Horner / Ah, that breed of dog. They have all the same tricks. They lie
down, roll over, suffer a beating, and still adore you for it. The
only difference being, the spaniel adores just the one master.

Sir Jasper / He! he! He!

Anita Quim / Oh the rude beast!

Dainty / Insolent brute!

Lady G / Stinking, rotten French bullock!

Sir Jasper / Now, now, ladies. −Shame on you, Master Horner! Your mother
was a woman
-Listen, dearest, you know you often need one more to make up
your jolly pack of card players, (low voice) and you can cheat
him easily for he's a rotten gambler.
(normal) Besides, you know you only have two old gentlemen
with not a tooth between them to escort you. Take a third into
your service.

Lady G / But are you sure he loves to play and has money?

Sir Jasper / He loves play as much as you, and has as much money as I.

Lady G / Then I am satisfied. Money, more than anything, makes up for
all other things lacking in a man.

Sir Jasper / Mr Horner, sir, I think perhaps it's high time you started keeping civil company, since you are now fit for it, and since you are lacking a lady to flatter and a good house to eat at, please frequent mine, where you can call my wife your 'mistress', and she will call you her 'flirt', as is the custom.

Horner / Who, me?

Sir Jasper / Indeed, for my sake. Come, for my sake.

Horner / For your sake?

Sir Jasper / Come, come, ladies, I have found a gambler for you here. Let him play with you sometimes, perhaps even be a little risqué. Let him play for ladies favours, you know.

Lady G / Only losing gamblers may have any favour with women.

Horner / On the contrary, madam. In my experience, the winning gambler has most favour with women. If a lady is willing to lose her money to a man, she'd be willing to lose anything else she has to offer, and afterwards the man may use her as he pleases.

Lady G / (interested) Really?

Sir Jasper / He! he! he! Well, win or lose, you shall have your liberty with her.

Lady G / Since he behaves himself now, for your sake I'll give him admittance and freedom.

Horner / Every sort of freedom, madam?

Sir Jasper / Aye, Aye, Aye, every freedom you can think of. So go with her, begin your new employment, charm her, amuse her, and be better acquainted with one another.
-Ladies, I have provided an innocent playfellow for you all there.

Dainty / Who, him?

Anita Quim / Foh! We'll have no such lewd playfellows, thank you very much.

Dainty / I think, sir, Anita has not heard the news.

Sir Jasper / Ah, then pray hear me out, Mrs Quim… (he whispers to her)

Anita Quim / (Gasps!) What? Lopped them right off?

Sir Jasper / Shhhh! (hushed) Don't let the poor fellow hear what we say!

Lady G / (turning to Horner) But, poor gentleman, you would allow yourself to suffer the greatest shame that could befall a man? So no shame could befall a woman of honour, such as I, if seen in conversation with you? To be known publicly as no longer a man?

Horner / You have my word, madam.

Lady G / (low voice, taking Horner aside) But, tell me sir, in confidence. Can you be as perfectly, perfectly manly as before your trip to France, sir? As perfectly, perfectly, sir?

Horner / (low voice) As perfectly, perfectly, madam. I don't ask you to take my word on it, allow me the chance to prove myself to you.

Lady G / (now interested) Well, that is spoken like a true man of honour. All men of honour desire to be tested. But, then again, you men generally say such things of yourselves anyway, one does not know what or whom to believe these days. However, sir, I find your case interests me deeply, and I have decided to abandon all caution and test you fully by placing myself in your more, I hope, than capable hands, dear, dear, noble sir.
So, in reply, I hereby willingly forfeit my honour for yours, at any time you should so desire, dear sir.

Horner / Dearest madam, you need not forfeit your honour for me, though I would willingly take it. I have given you the security to save yours from harm. My late condition being so well known to the world.

Lady G / But what if - upon any future falling-out - you yourself should betray your trust, dear sir? What I mean is - if you'll give me leave to speak openly and obscenely - you might tell others our dishonourable secret, dear sir.

Horner / Even if I did, nobody would believe me. The reputation of impotency is rarely recovered from, like that of cowardice, dear madam.

Lady G / Well then, as one might say, you may do your worst, dear, dear sir.

Sir Jasper / Come, come. Have you agreed on matters? I must leave for Whitehall.

Lady G / Why, indeed, Sir Jasper, Master Horner is a thousand times a better man than I thought him before. Truly, not long ago, I thought his very name an obscenity, and to name him as a friend would have been as likely as my permitting him to lay with me!

Dainty / Sister!

Anita Quim / Oh my!

Sir Jasper / He! He! Well, your ladyship is as virtuous as any woman I know, and all the town knows about him - he! he! he! Therefore, now you like him you may go to your pleasure together while I see to my business.

Lady G / Come, then, dear 'flirt'.

Horner / (offers arm) With pleasure, dearest 'mistress'.

Sir Jasper / (leaving) Good, good. It's just the way I would have it.

Horner / (aside) And just the way I'd have it.

End of Act II

ACT III

ACT III SCENE I. MR PINCHWIFE'S LODGINGS

[ALITHEA AND MRS PINCHWIFE ARE TALKING]

Alithea / Sister, what ails you? You seem depressed.

Mrs Pinch / Oh Alithea, it would make anyone depressed to stay at home since my husband told me what lives the London ladies live while out and about. With their dancing, and dressing up, and playing at nine-pins every day of the week, so they do.

[ENTER MR PINCHWIFE]

Mr Pinch / What's going on here? Are you putting the idea of town-pleasures into her head again, and setting her a longing.

Alithea / (sarcastic) Yes, brother, with nine-pin bowling.

Mr Pinch / The liberty you take wandering abroad makes her hanker after it. Poor wretch!

Alithea / Oh, and she asks whether she may have your permission to enjoy a walk in the park.

Mr Pinch / A walk? In the park? She has been in town all week, and until this afternoon had no desire to venture abroad.

Alithea / Was she not at a play yesterday?

Mr Pinch / Yes, but she never asked to go. I chose for her to go myself.

Alithea / Then if she asks to go out, you are the cause of her asking, not my example.

Mr Pinch / Well, the day after tomorrow, before it is light we'll be rid of this town. (to wife) Come, dearest, don't be sad, you'll be back in the country after tomorrow.

Mrs Pinch / Pish! Why do you have to remind me of the country?

Mr Pinch / What's this! What? Pish at the country?

Mrs Pinch / Leave me alone. I am not well.

Mr Pinch / Not well? Of what illness?

Mrs Pinch / Truly, I don't know, but I have not been well since you told me there was a gentleman at the play in love with me.

Mr Pinch / So! You are not well because a lewd fellow chanced to lie and say he liked you.

Mrs Pinch / Please, dear, let us go to a play to-night.

Mr Pinch / But you have been already. Why are you so eager to see a play?

Mrs Pinch / In truth, dearest, I care not one pin for the play, but I would like to see the gentleman who said he loves me.

Alithea / And I'm the cause of men's desires too, I suppose!

Mr Pinch / Now I think of it, yes. Who was the cause of Horner coming to my lodgings today? It was you.

Alithea / No, it was you, because you would not let him see your pretty little wife outside of your lodgings.

Mrs Pinch / Oh Lord! Did the gentleman really come here to see me?

Mr Pinch / No, no. Mistress Alithea was the real reason for his visit. (almost aside) And once we are back in the country we will be rid of all this curiosity, I know the ways of this town. Yesterday he broke his carriage wheel near our house, on purpose I'm sure. I am no fool.

Mrs Pinch / Come, please, husband, let's go out somewhere before it is too late.

Mr Pinch / No.

Mrs Pinch / [stamping foot] I will go out, I am telling you now!

Mr Pinch / So! Already the obstinacy of a town-wife I see. I will not take you out where you can be seen and known.

Alithea / You could put a mask on her.

Mr Pinch / Pshaw! A mask makes people all the more inquisitive, and is as ridiculous a disguise as a stage beard. If we should meet Horner, he would insist on joining us, and start talking to her, and leering at her, and the devil knows what else. No, I'll not have her wear a mask, it is too dangerous.

Mrs Pinch / Well? Shall we go? The Exchange will be shut soon, and I have a mind to see that.

Mr Pinch / I have it. I'll dress her in the suit we have to carry down to her younger brother. That will mask her beauty. See, I understand the town-tricks.

Alithea / I once had a gentleman admirer who would say,
    "A beauty masked, like the sun in eclipse,
     Gathers more gazers, than when fully lit".
-Hurry along and dress her, we'll be late.

ACT III SCENE II. THE NEW EXCHANGE. EARLY EVENING

With the closeness of Covent Garden and Lincoln's Inn Fields, and the loss of the Royal Exchange in the Great Fire, the New Exchange became a very fashionable place to shop, and to socialize: references to it in Restoration comedy are almost obligatory. It was also famed for it's excellent book shops.
The New Exchange was divided into four sections, with an "Outer Walk" and "Inner Walk" on each of the two floors ("Above" or "Below Stairs"). The lower floor had a reputation as a place for romantic assignations. People are dressed ready for the evening entertainment of a stroll, the theatre or dining.

[ENTER HORNER, HANCOCK, AND UPPINGTON]

Uppington / Not supping with us, Horner?

Horner / I have a prior engagement.

Uppington / Women stealing you away from us?

Horner / Aye, a pox on 'em all!

Hancock / My, how you've changed. You really hate them now you have no use for them. Why do you keep company with them?

Horner / I keep company with them so I can hate them even more. Nothing makes a man hate a woman more than her constant conversation, ask any married man.

Uppington / The sly old fox must have some other motive. Dining with women he cannot lie with? That's like dining with a rich fool he cannot cheat.

Horner / I have known you dine with a fool, Uppington, just to share his wine.

Hancock / His wine or his wife? (laughs)

Uppington / But Horner, leaving our company? And for society women too!

Horner / You know it is lawful for a man to leave his drinking companions for a wench.

Uppington / But, only to drink with the wench?

Horner / Who would want the company of a sober whore?

Hancock / Do the society ladies drink then?

Horner / Yes, Hancock, at least I still have the pleasure of laying them flat with a bottle.

Hancock / Foh! Drinking with women is as unnatural as meaningful conversation with them.

Uppington / Unless you are an old fornicator looking for pleasure.

Hancock / No, no. Riches! A woman will behave however you like if you offer her money and title.

Horner / Whereas she'll 'misbehave' however you like after two bottles of fine champagne, and you can be rid of her in the morning.

Hancock / Foh! Wine and women, good apart, together as nauseous as a sack of sugar.
-But a little of your advice before you go, Horner - you see, I have designs on women other than eating and drinking with them. Or at least, one woman in particular. I am in love with the foolish Count's mistress, the trouble being, he is marrying her tomorrow.

[ENTER SPARKISH, LOOKING ABOUT]

Horner / Well, here comes just the one who could help you, Hancock.

Hancock / Him? Sparkish is my rival, he would hinder my love.

Horner / Not at all. A jealous husband is the best assistance a rival can have.

Hancock / How so?

Horner / He will forbid his wife from seeing his rival. And you know what they say about forbidden fruit.

Hancock / But I can't get near his mistress except in his company.

Horner / All the better for you. The best way to rob a fool of his goods, is to keep his company.

Sparkish / [approaching] Who is to be robbed? Goodness, let me join in. I haven't met with a robber since Christmas.

Hancock / (jokingly) Didn't you hear? We were talking about you of course.

Sparkish / Ha! Ha! Ha! Come, you robbing rogues, where shall we dine?
-Oh, Hancock, my mistress tells me you were flirting madly with her last night all through the play. Ha! ha! -But I...

Hancock / I? Flirting with her?

Sparkish / Well, I forgive you, I am sure you meant no harm by it.

Hancock / Did she tell you this? I think you'll find women are apt to enhance the value of their worth by wildly exaggerating offers made to them.

Horner / Aye, women are apt to talk before the intrigue, men talk after it, proof by far they are the vainer sex. Though, if I were a mistress of Sparky, I think I'd be desperate for some intrigue.

Sparkish / By my word, sir, are you teasing me? And it's SparkEESH. Count SparkEESH. But talking of teasing, I saw you at the play yesterday. The wits were being rather bold with you, sir. Did you not hear us laugh?

Horner / I did. But I was foolishly under the impression that people went to plays to laugh at the playwright's wit, not at their own.

Sparkish / Upon my oath, no thank you, sir! 'Gad, I go to a play as I go to a country retreat. I carry my own wine to one, and my own wit to the other, else I would not be merry at either.

Uppington / Hey, look who's coming, Sparky.

[ENTER MR PINCHWIFE WITH MRS PINCHWIFE IN
MEN'S CLOTHES, ALITHEA AND LUCY]

Sparkish / What? Oh, hide me! My mistress is with them. Stand in front of me.

[SPARKISH HIDES HIMSELF BEHIND HANCOCK]

Hancock / Too late. She's seen you.

Sparkish / But I don't want to see her. It's time to go to Whitehall, I must not miss the drawing-room chatter.

Hancock / Introduce me first, I fear she may still hate me.

Sparkish / Another time. Goodness, the king will have dined already.

Hancock / And be no worse of stomach for your absence. You are one of those fools who think their attendance at the king's meals is because they make good company.

Sparkish / Pshaw! I know my company is of great interest, sir. Quick hide me.

Horner / (calls out) Pinchwife! Join us!

Sparkish / (hiding behind Hancock's coat) No, no! Don't call them over here.

[THE PINCHWIFES CONTINUE TO WALK PAST STALLS SELLING GOODS]

[HANCOCK DELIBERATELY STEPS TO ONE SIDE AS IF TO SEE BETTER, REVEALING SPARKISH WHO QUICKLY STEPS BEHIND HANCOCK AGAIN, WHO THEN PROMPTLY STEPS THE OTHER WAY AGAIN PRETENDING HE IS NOT AWARE OF THE CHARADE TAKING PLACE BEHIND HIM]

Horner / What? He pretends not to know us!

Mr Pinch / (ushering his wife) Come along, wife.

Mrs Pinch / I thought I was to be my brother this evening.
-Oh, bookseller, do you have any ballads? Give me sixpenny worth.

Bookseller / We have no ballads, madam.

Mrs Pinch / (indignant that he has not noticed her disguise) Sir! If you don't mind. Then give me a copy of "A Covent Garden Madam" and a maybe a play.
-Oh, here's one; "The Knocking Shop And The Slighted Maiden". That sounds manly, I'll take it.

Mr Pinch / (concerned at the content) No, dear brother, plays are not for your reading.
(aside to wife) Come along, do you want to be discovered?

Horner / Who is that youth with him, Sparky?

Sparkish / (looking around the side of Hancock) It could be his wife's brother, because he's something like her. I have only seen her the once though, and she was adorably young. Stay still Hancock!

Horner / Extremely handsome. I have seen a face like it too. Let us follow them.

[PINCHWIFE, MRS PINCHWIFE, ALITHEA, AND LUCY CARRY ON WALKING. HORNER AND UPPINGTON FOLLOW THEM. SPARKISH STAYS BEHIND AND HANCOCK STOPS FOR HIM.]

Hancock / Come on, Count, your lady saw you and will be angry you do not go to her. Besides, I need you with me in order to be reconciled with her, dear friend.

Sparkish / Well, that gives me good reason, dear Hancock. I would not go to her now, for her sake or my own, but for an old friend, I couldn't possibly say no.

Hancock / I am obliged to you indeed, dear friend. I would be friends with her, only to be friends with you still. I find these ties to wives usually dissolve all ties to friends.

Sparkish / Never worry, dear friend. I'll be divorced from her sooner than from you. Come on, but I can't stay long.

[THEY TURN AND MAKE TOWARDS THE OTHERS]

[MR AND MRS PINCHWIFE WALK SLOWLY OFF, MRS PINCHWIFE PUTTING ON AN EXAGGERATED SLOW MALE SWAGGER. ALITHEA HANGS BACK IN THE HOPE THAT SPARKISH WILL NOTICE AND JOIN HER]

Mr Pinch / (calling back to Alithea) Sister, if you will not come, we must leave you here.
-(Aside to wife) The foolish woman will muster up all the young idlers of this place to introduce to us, the swarm of cuckold-makers they are! Come on, Margery, let's be gone from here.

Mrs Pinch / (excited, dropping into country, losing her airs and graces) Not likely. I han't half my bellyful of sights yet.

Mr Pinch / (seeing the men heading for them) Then let us at least stand away from them.

Mrs Pinch / Lord, what a wealth of bold signs there are here! Rooms available by the hour at the Bull's-Head, the Ram's-Head, and the Stag's-Head.

Mr Pinch / And if every husband's proper sign were visible here, they would be all much the same.

Mrs Pinch / What d'ye mean by that, dearest?

Mr Pinch / Their signs would all be Bulls, Stags, and Rams. Come along.

[THE PINCHWIFES EXIT – SPARKISH & HANCOCK JOIN ALITHEA & LUCY]

Sparkish / Alithea, my dear, for my sake, make up and be friends with Hancock again.

Alithea / For your sake? It's because of you I hate him.

Hancock / That is something too cruel, madam, to hate me because of him.

Sparkish / Aye indeed, madam, too cruel to me as well, to hate my friend because of me.

Alithea / I hate him because he is your enemy. If you loved me you should hate him too for attempting to make love to me.

Sparkish / That is your fault not his.

Alithea / How is it my fault?

Sparkish / For being so desirable.

Alithea / Are you not concerned for my honour? Allowing a man to make love to me, the day before our wedding?

Sparkish / If he makes love to you it is a sign you are attractive. The fact I am not jealous is a sign you are virtuous and I have trust in you. That I think is a sign you are honourable.

Alithea / You astonish me, Count, with your lack of jealousy. Are you not afraid to lose me?

Sparkish / 'Gad, I see virtue makes a woman as troublesome as a little reading and learning.

Alithea / That is preposterous! I'm telling you straight, he pursues me to marry me.

Sparkish / Pshaw!

Hancock / Come, madam, you can see you strive in vain to make him jealous of me. My dear friend is the kindest creature in the world to me.

Sparkish / Yes, dear fellow!

Hancock / I would not wrong him nor you for the world.

Alithea / Pshaw! (She turns away)

Sparkish / Look here. Hear him out. Don't walk away.

Hancock / Yes, I would not want to see you cast yourself away upon so unworthy and inconsiderate a thing as you see here.

Sparkish / No, no, dear friend.
-Madam, you can see, he would rather wrong himself than me.

Alithea / You fool, can't you see he's talking about you? I can no longer suffer his scurrilous abuse towards you, nor will I stand his attempts of love towards me.

[SHE TURNS TO GO. SPARKISH TAKES HOLD OF HER ARM]

Sparkish / By the world! Can a man not speak civilly to a woman nowadays, without her accusing him of making love to her?
Nay, madam, you shall stay, - I insist - at least until he has explained his love for you.
-Now, explain yourself, my friend. How do you love my mistress here?

Hancock / With all my soul.

Alithea / I thank him. At last I thinks he speaks plainly enough for any fool to see.

Sparkish / You still do not understand. -But with what kind of love, Hancock?

Hancock / With the finest and the truest love in the world.

Sparkish / See! That is not matrimonial love.

Alithea / What? Are you saying matrimonial love is not the finest?

Sparkish / 'Gad, did I ever go too far without thinking.
-But explain yourself, Hancock, you said you would not wrong
me.

Hancock / No, no, madam, I would not wrong the man...
[Claps his hand to his breast] ...who should by rights be yours...

Sparkish / Look, there you are, madam.

Hancock / ...He that loves you most...

Alithea / Look, Count. Who do you think he means?

Sparkish / Who else could it be? -Go on, Hancock.

Hancock / (continuing) ...who loves you more than titles or fortune chasing
fools...

[POINTS AT SPARKISH]

Sparkish / See there, he means me still, he points at me.

Alithea / I am beginning to understand his point.

Hancock / ...who loves you better even than his own self.

Sparkish / Aye. - No, madam, indeed, you shan't go until at least until you
have made up with him after his honest declaration of affection
just now.

Alithea / Have a care, you may regret making me stay so long.

[RE-ENTER MR AND MRS PINCHWIFE]

Sparkish / Come, I pray, madam, be friends with him again, kiss and embrace him fondly

Alithea / You must pardon me, sir, that I am not yet so obedient to you.

Mr Pinch / What? Inviting your wife to kiss men, Count? Monstrous! Are you not ashamed?

Sparkish / Are you not ashamed, Mr Pinchwife, that I should have more confidence in the chastity of your family than you seem to have? I am a man of honour, sir, an open man.

Mr Pinch / Very open, sir, to share your wife with your friends.

Sparkish / He is a humble, well meaning friend. The type that reconciles the differences of the marriage bed. You know that man and wife do not always agree.

Mr Pinch / You will get a great many well meaning friends by sharing your wife as you do, Sparkish.

Sparkish / What if I do? It may be that I get pleasure from it, like I do showing fine clothes at a play-house, or counting money in front of poor rogues.

Mr Pinch / Any fool who shows off his wife and money risks losing both.

Sparkish / I love to be envied, and to tell you the truth, it may be that I love to have rivals in my wife. They make her seem more like a kept mistress. —Which reminds me, I must bid you a good night, for I am due at Whitehall.

Alithea / Pah!

[ALITHEA TURNS HER BACK ON THE MEN AND STEPS AWAY IN A DISPLAY OF SHUNNING THEM, ANSWERING THE GOODNIGHT FROM SPARKISH WITH A FLICK OF HER HAND OVER HER SHOULDER]

Sparkish / Madam Alithea, I hope you are now reconciled with my good friend. Therefore, I wish you a good night, my dearest, and good sleep if you can. Tomorrow, as you know, I visit you early with a gentleman of the cloth. -Good night, dear Hancock.

Hancock /   Good night, Sparky. I will do my best to help relations with your wife.

[EXIT SPARKISH]

Sparkish /   (as he walks away) SparkEESH!

Lucy /   (aside to Hancock) What easy-going husbands women of quality can meet! A poor chambermaid like me could never have such lady-like luck. He's wasted on her, she'll not take advantage of her good fortune – he's a pure bred cuckold if ever I saw one, and you don't find many of them about.

Hancock /   (aside to Lucy) I am sure a woman such as yourself would take advantage of fortune put her way. Especially if it saved a lady from being wasted on such a wretch as the Count.

Lucy /   (aside to Harcourt) How much fortune would a woman need to prevent such a waste?

Hancock /   Ooh, about five hundred, I would say.

Lucy /   Done.

Hancock /   Good.

Hancock /   (sidling up close, slyly speaking) Alithea, dearest Madam, I am hoping you will not do me the dishonour of turning me away to-morrow morning, should I happen to call on you earlier than Count Sparkish with my own gentleman of the cloth.

[PINCHWIFE COMES BETWEEN ALITHEA AND HANCOCK]

Mr Pinch /   Stand away! This woman is still under my care, sir, therefore you must restrain your freedom with her, sir.

Hancock /   Must, sir?

Mr Pinch /   Yes, sir. She is my sister, sir.

Hancock / Then you are a lucky man, sir, for I am merely her servant. (bows) Madam.

Mr Pinch / Come away, sister. We would had been gone if it had not been for you, and so avoided these lewd rake-hells.

[RE-ENTER HORNER AND UPPINGTON HEADING FOR PINCHWIFE]

Mr Pinch / And as if one was not enough! Still they come.

Horner / Ah, Pinchwife! How's things?

Mr Pinch / (curt) Horner.

Horner / What? I see a little time in the country turns a man wild and unsociable, fit only to converse with his horses, dogs, and turds.

Mr Pinch / I have business, sir, and must mind it. Your business is pleasure, therefore you and I must go different ways.

Horner / Well, you may go on, but this pretty young gentleman should stay with us.

Mr Pinch / 'Sdeath!

Horner / (to Mrs Pinchwife, taking her arm). Would you not rather stay with us, young sir?
—Tell me, Pinchwife, who is this pretty young gentleman?

Mr Pinch / One to whom I am a guardian, and one I would wish to keep out of your hands.

Horner / Who is he? I never saw anything so pretty in all my life.

Mr Pinch / Pshaw! Do not look at him that way, he's a poor bashful youth, you'll put him out of countenance. -Come away, brother.

[GOES TO TAKE HER AWAY]

Horner / Oh, he's your brother!

Mr Pinch / Yes, well, my wife's brother. -Come, come, she's a supper waiting for us.

Horner / I thought so! For he is very like her. I saw you at the play with her, she was the one I told you I was in love with.

Mrs Pinch / Oh Jiminy! Is it him that was in love with me? - I mean her. He's a curiously fine gentleman, and I would love him too if I were a sister. Is this him, brother?

Mr Pinch / Come on, come away.

Horner / Why the haste, Pinchwife? Why won't you let him talk with us?

Mr Pinch / Because you'll debauch him. He's still young and innocent, and I would not have him debauched for anything in the world. See how he gazes on you already? The little devil!

Horner / Hancock, Uppington, look here, this is the likeness of his wife. That dowdy he was telling us about. Did you ever see a lovelier creature? The rogue has every reason to be jealous of his wife if she is like him.

Hancock / And, as I remember now, she is as like him as can be.

Uppington / She is indeed very pretty if she is like him.

Horner / She is a glorious creature, beautiful beyond all things I ever beheld.

Mr Pinch / (getting frustrated) Yes, yes, now gentlemen if you please…

Horner / More beautiful than the finest mistress I ever laid with.

Mrs Pinch / Nay, now you mock, sir. I must ask you not to mock me.

Horner / I speak of your sister, young sir.

Mr Pinch / Aye, but saying she was pretty if she looked like him made him blush.

Horner / I think he is so pretty he should not be a man.

Mr Pinch / Come, let him go, we can stay fooling no longer. His sister has supper ready for us.

Horner / Does she? Come then, we'll all go to supper with you both.

Mr Pinch / No, now I think of it, having waited so long for us, I warrant she's gone to bed.
(to his wife.) Come, I rise early tomorrow, come along.

Horner / (bawdy) How fortunate for your wife. Well then, if she has gone to bed, I wish her and you a good night. But pray, young gentleman, present my humble greetings to her.

Mrs Pinch / Thank you heartily, sir.

[SHE DOES A LITTLE CURTSEY]

Mr Pinch / (Hissed aside to Mrs Pinchwife) 'Sdeath, don't curtsey! Do you wish to reveal yourself to spite me?

Horner / Tell her, dear sweet young gentleman, despite your brother there, that you have revived the love I had for her at first sight in the playhouse.

Mrs Pinch / Did you love her? Indeed and indeed?

Horner / Yes, indeed and indeed. Pray, do tell her so, and give her this kiss from me.

[HE KISSES HER ON THE LIPS]

Mr Pinch / Sir, I must insist you do not kiss my brother!

Mrs Pinch / Why do you kiss me? I am no woman.

Mr Pinch / Come, I cannot and will not stay any longer.

Horner / Good night, dear young gentleman. And ladies, good night, farewell.

Mrs Pinch / Good night indeed, gentlemen.

[HORNER, HANCOCK, AND UPPINGTON WANDER AWAY]

Mr Pinch / So, they are gone at last. Insufferable man! We must leave too. Stay here, I'll see that the coach is ready.

Mrs Pinch / Yes, dearest.

[EXIT MR PINCHWIFE. MRS PINCHWIFE STANDS STARING AT THE SIGHTS AROUND HER]

Mrs Pinch / Lucy, it is so much fun to be in the town I find. I feel like a new woman!

Lucy / And so do most of the married men-folk here. Ha ha!

Mrs Pinch / (dreamily) It would be so delicious to be a city-wife.

[MRS PINCHWIFE STOPS SUDDENLY WITH A THOUGHT. HORNER, HANCOCK, AND UPPINGTON SAUNTER BACK HAVING SEEN PINCHWIFE LEAVE]

Horner / What, not gone yet? Will you be sure to do as I asked, sweet sir?

Mrs Pinch / (scampishly swinging her arms) I may sir. What will you give me in return?

Horner / Anything you like. Come into the next walkway, I'll show you. Come on.

[EXIT HORNER, WITH HIS ARM AROUND MRS PINCHWIFE, GUIDING HER]

Alithea / Wait! Wait! Where are you going?

Hancock / Relax, madam, he's only gone to show him something - he'll be back shortly.

[HANCOCK PREVENTS ALITHEA FOLLOWING BY PLACING HIS ARM AROUND HER]

Hancock / Anyway, I can't let you go till you've answered my question. Alithea my dear…

Alithea / (pushing him away) Pray let me go, sir. I have said and suffered enough already.

Lucy / For God's sake, I'd best follow 'em.

> [UPPINGTON, LIKEWISE, PUTS HIS ARM AROUND LUCY PREVENTING HER FOLLOWING]

Uppington / You stay here, you strapping creature. And it is no use struggling, so save your strength for later and show me a little fondness. Like a little kiss…

> [UPPINGTON TRIES TO KISS LUCY, SHE TURNS HER HEAD AWAY, BUT SHE LOOKS PLEASED AT THE ATTENTION]

Lucy / Get orf me! Believe me, I have taken on bigger men that you in my time, sir.

Uppington / Do not judge a book by it's cover, madam. I have hidden depths, let me show you.

> [THE LADIES STRUGGLE WITH THE MEN AS MR PINCHWIFE RETURNS]

Mr Pinch / Where? How? Gone? Where?

Lucy / She…he's gone with the gentleman to show him something, if it pleases your worship.

Mr Pinch / Something! Show him something? With a pox he will! Where are they?

Alithea / Only in the next walkway, brother.

Mr Pinch / Only, only! Where, where? I must find them!

> [MR PINCHWIFE EXITS HURRIEDLY, RETURNS, LOOKS, THEN GOES OUT AGAIN]

Hancock /   What is the matter with him? Why is he so concerned? But, dearest madam…

Alithea /   Sir, I must insist you restrain yourself, and leave me in peace.

Hancock /   Have you no pity for my sufferings?

Alithea /   To suffer them when they were not my doing was cruelty, you'll get no pity from me. I never wish to see you ever again.

Hancock /   Then, madam, let me take my right as the banished lover, of giving you a farewell reason why you should not marry my rival tomorrow.

Alithea /   Since I am engaged to him, he, and only he, can give me reason why I should not marry him. As he is true to me, and I truly believe he is, I must be true to him. So good night, sir.

Hancock /   Are women faithful only because their husbands are, and like fortune only married to fools?

[RE-ENTER PINCHWIFE]

Mr Pinch /   (frantic) Gone, gone, I can't find them! Quite gone! Ten thousand plagues on them! Which way did they go?

Alithea /   Only to the other walk, brother.

Lucy /   I'm sure their business will soon be done, if it pleases your worship. It can't take long doing, I'm sure of it.

Alithea /   Are they not there?

Mr Pinch /   No! You know where they are, you infamous wretch! As if you do not bring enough dishonour on your family by yourself, you have to help her do it. You legion of bawds!

Alithea /   My goodness, brother!

Lucy /   Look! Here she comes now.

[RE-ENTER MRS PINCHWIFE RUNNING, WITH HER
HANDS FULL OF GIFTS AND DRIED FRUIT UNDER
HER ARM, HORNER FOLLOWING]

Mrs Pinch / Oh dearest, look what I have got, see!

Mr Pinch / (rubbing his head) What have I got you into here?

Mrs Pinch / The fine gentleman here has given me lovely things.

Mr Pinch / Has he indeed? Perhaps that's why he is so breathless and ruddy.

Horner / I have only given your young brother a gift, sir.

Mr Pinch / And that is all you have given I hope.

[ENTER SIR JASPER GOODING AT PACE,
RESCUING PINCHWIFE]

Sir Jasper / Ah, Master Horner. Come, come with me, the ladies will excuse
you I am sure. Your mistress, my wife that is, wonders why you
do not make haste to her.

Horner / I have waited a good half hour here for you, it is your fault I am
not with your wife.

Sir Jasper / (guiltily) Oh, yes, well, I must ask you not to let her know as
much. The truth of it is, I was advancing a certain project to his
majesty…

Horner / I am sure you have a hundred valid excuses lined up, so come, let's
go, you can tell your wife when we get to your house. Good night,
sweet young gentleman.
(leaving) Come on, let's not keep the lady waiting.

Sir Jasper / Good day, sirs, and madams.

[EXIT SIR JASPER GOODING AND HORNER]

Uppington / There is no justice in the world, Hancock. Horner may have the
privileges, but he can't make good use of them. And I'd wager on
Lady Gooding being a feisty mare.

Hancock / Aye, to poor Horner it's like coming into an inheritance in old age, just when a man can't take advantage of it.

Uppington / Come on, let's get us a bite to eat, we will need our energy for later.
(to Alithea) Madam Alithea, your servant.
(to Lucy bawdily) And a good night, strapper!

Lucy / Really!

Hancock / Madam Alithea, though you will give me neither a good day or night, I still wish you a good day. I dare not mention the other half of my wish.

Alithea / Then I will. I wish you good night, sir. For ever.

[THE MEN SAUNTER OFF]

Mrs Pinch / I don't know where to put this gift, dearest, perhaps you should look after it.

Mr Pinch / Indeed, I shall.

[STRIKES AWAY THE GIFT]

Mrs Pinch / Dearest, what's a eunuch?

Mr Pinch / What? A fruit from the plantain plant I think. Long and thick.

Mrs Pinch / Interesting.

Mr Pinch / Why do you ask?

Mrs Pinch / Oh nothing. I heard someone referred to as one earlier.

[HE LOOKS AT HER ODDLY, AND THEY EXIT]

End of Act III

Intermission

ACT IV

ACT IV SCENE I. MR PINCHWIFE'S LODGINGS NEXT MORNING

[LUCY IS DRESSING ALITHEA IN WEDDING
CLOTHES]

Lucy / (who has been bribed by Hancock to win over Alithea)
There, madam, all dressed and ready. You are set about with so
many ornaments and ounces of perfume that I am reminded of
readying a corpse for a second hand grave rather than Count
Sparkish's bed. (low) Though I doubt you'll find much more life in
either.

Alithea / Hold your peace, Lucy.

Lucy / But madam, why did you banish poor Mr Hancock forever from
your sight? How could you be so hard-hearted?

Alithea / It was because I was not hard-hearted.

Lucy / (sarcastic) Oh, no. 'Twas clearly love and affection.

Alithea / It was. I could see him no more, because I love him I think.

Lucy / My, my. That's sound reasoning!

Alithea / You do not understand me.

Lucy / I don't think you understand yourself.

Alithea / I was already engaged to marry another, whom my good heart and
decency would not allow me to deceive.

Lucy / Can there be a greater deceit than to give a man your person without your heart? Have you no conscience?

Alithea / I'll retrieve it for him after I am married a while. My heart that is.

Lucy / A lady who marries to love better is no better than a wench who marries to live better.

Alithea / What are you saying?

Lucy / They both soon find their bed empty at night. Marrying to find love, madam, is like gambling to find riches. You only lose what little stock you had to start.

Alithea / I suspect from your words you have been bribed to betray me.

Lucy / Oh no. Bribed only by the goodness of the man who seduced your heart, or would have done if not for your rigid honour. But what a devil this honour is! The things it makes us do. 'Tis surely a disease in the head.

Alithea / No, man lives by honour.

Lucy / Yes. And man dies by it, but not women, madam, they live for love, love is our life, and if you miss love, you miss life. It's not too late to reconsider Mr Hancock you know.

Alithea / Enough, no more talk of honour, nor of Mr Hancock.
-I wish the Count would hurry up and secure my honour and his right to have me and hold me.

Lucy / You will marry him then?

Alithea / Certainly. I have given him my word already, and will give my hand too when he comes.

Lucy / Or your mouth.

Alithea / Whatever do you mean?

Lucy / You swear an oath, give your word, and give yourself with a kiss. 'Tis all mouth, that's what gentleman want. -But is he not a little naïve compared to the other fine gentleman?

Alithea / I admit he lacks the wit of Hancock, but I can happily live with that on account of another lacking it leads to. That of jealousy, which men of wit seldom lack.

Lucy / Lord, madam, what would you be doing to make him jealous? You intend to be honest don't you? Trust is the most important marriage virtue, once thrown away it can never be retrieved.

Alithea / If he has cause to suspect my virtue, then he should be jealous. It's only his blind confidence in my virtue that obliges me to be so faithful to him.

Lucy / Are you sure his confidence will last?

Alithea / I am satisfied it is impossible for him to be jealous after the proof I have seen of him. And jealousy in a husband? - Heaven defend me from it! It brings a thousand plagues to a poor woman, the loss of her honour, her peace and quiet, and her...

Lucy / Pleasure?

Alithea / What do you mean? Are you being impertinent?

Lucy / Liberty is a great pleasure, madam.

Alithea / As I was saying... loss of her honour, her peace and quiet, and, even worse - her life, when she is sent into the country. It is as terrible a place as a monastery for our young English ladies.

Lucy / I'd rather my innocence went to a London jailer, than a country squire, not that they'd have me of course. (afterthought) Or that I have any innocence left to give.

Alithea / Formerly women of society married fools for a great estate and a fine country seat. Nowadays a man must have a title and a pretty seat in Lincoln's Inn Fields or Covent Garden.

[ENTER SPARKISH WITH HANCOCK DRESSED AS A PARSON]

Sparkish / Madam, your humble servant. A happy day to you, and to us all.

Hancock / Amen.

Alithea / At last, Count. And Hancock? What are you doing here?

Sparkish / My chaplain. In good faith, madam, poor Hancock offers his warmest regards, and in obedience to your last commands, refrains from coming into your sight.

Alithea / Is that not him?

Sparkish / No, fy, no. But to show that he never intended to hinder our match, he has sent his brother here to join our hands. According to custom, to get me a wife, I must get me a chaplain. This here is his brother, and my chaplain.

Alithea / His brother!

Sparkish / And your chaplain.

Alithea / His brother!

Sparkish / See, I knew she would not believe it. I told you, sir, she would take you for your brother Frank.

Alithea / Believe it!

Lucy / His brother, Frank! ha! ha! he! He still has a trick left, it seems.

Sparkish / Come, my dearest, pray let us go to church before the canonical hour is past.

Alithea / To your shame, you are being abused by him still.

Sparkish / I cannot believe you are being so sceptical.

Alithea / I cannot believe you are being so gullible.

Sparkish / Dearest of my life, hear me out. I tell you this is Ned Hancock of Cambridge. By the world, you can see he has a sneaking college look. 'Tis true he's something like his brother Frank, in fact they differ from each other in nothing more than their age, being twins.

Lucy / Ha! ha! ha!

Alithea / I am not so easily deceived as you. So tell me, how do you know what you claim so confidently is true?

Sparkish / Why I'll tell you. Frank Hancock came to me this morning to wish me joy, and offer his services in any way he could. I asked him if he could help me find a parson. Whereupon he told me he had a brother in town who was in holy orders, and he went straight away and sent him to me, as you see here.

Alithea / So, Frank goes and puts on a black coat, then tells you he is Ned.

Sparkish / Pshaw! pshaw! I tell you, the parson told me the midwife put her garter around Frank's neck to tell them apart, they were so alike.

Alithea / Frank tells you this too?

Sparkish / Aye, Frank and Ned. Well, they are both part of the same story.

Alithea / So, very, very foolish.

Sparkish / Lord, if you won't believe me, you had best run him by your chambermaid there. For chambermaids know chaplains from other men, they are so used to them.

Lucy / (examining him) Let's see. Well, I'll swear he has the canonical smirk, and the filthy clammy palm of a chaplain.

Alithea / Well, *'most reverend'* sir, let us put an end to this fooling.

Hancock / With all my soul, divine heavenly creature, whenever you please.

Alithea / (to Sparkish) And this is how a chaplain speaks is it?

Sparkish / Why, was there not *soul, divine* and *heavenly*, in what he said?

Alithea / Once more, most impertinent black coat, cease your persecution and let us put an end to this troublesome affair, I have no patience left.

Hancock / So be it, serene lady, when your honour should think it right and convenient so to do.

Sparkish / 'Gad, I'm sure only a chaplain could speak that way.

Alithea / Let me tell you, sir, this dull trick will not serve your cause. You may delay our marriage, but you will not hinder it.

Hancock / Far be it from me, munificent patroness, to delay your marriage. I desire nothing more than to marry you, which I would do this instant, if you yourself, or my noble, good-natured, and thrice generous patron here, would not hinder it.

Sparkish / No, indeed, not I.

Hancock / And now, madam, let me tell you plainly, nobody else shall marry you, by Heavens, I'd die first if they did!

Alithea / And that was spoken like a chaplain too was it? Now you understand him, I hope.

Lucy / How his devotion has made him forget his function - as I have seen in real parsons!

Sparkish / Poor man, he feels insulted to be refused. I can't blame him, it is putting an indignity upon him which should not have to be suffered. So, if you'll pardon me, madam, it shan't be. He shall marry us. Come along if you please, hurry, madam.

Lucy / Ha! ha! he! More ado! It's almost too late now.

Alithea / Complete stupidity! I tell you, he would marry me as your rival, not as your chaplain.

Sparkish / [pulling her away] Come, come on, madam.

Lucy / Ha, ha! Do not refuse this reverend divine the honour and satisfaction of marrying you, madam. For I dare say, he has his heart set on it.

Alithea / And what do you hope to gain by this, Lucy?

Sparkish / Come, madam, it's almost twelve o'clock, and my mother warned me never to be married out of canonical hours. Come, come, Lord, it's just first day modesty and nerves, nothing more.

Lucy / Oh yes, married women are only modest the first day - because married men are only loving the first day.

ACT IV SCENE II. A CHAMBER IN MR PINCHWIFE'S LODGINGS.

[MR AND MRS PINCHWIFE ARE PRESENT. SHE IS SITTING WHILE HE IS PACING ABOUT THE ROOM IN FRUSTRATION]

Mr Pinch / Come on, tell me I say. What happened next?

Mrs Pinch / Lord, what pleasure you take in hearing it, for sure!

Mr Pinch / Not as much as the pleasure you take in telling it, I find. Now, what happened next?

Mrs Pinch / He carried me up into the house next to the Exchange.

Mr Pinch / So, only the two of you were in the room.

Mrs Pinch / Yes, he sent away a youth who was there for some dried fruit and some trinkets.

Mr Pinch / Did he indeed, damn him! -and then?

Mrs Pinch / Then the lady of the house came up.

Mr Pinch / It was just as well she did. What did she have to say?

Mrs Pinch / She said I was very handsome for a boy, more handsome even than the girls she had working for her. She said the pretty working girls earned more money, and they didn't have to try as hard to earn a living.

Mr Pinch / What kind of house was this?

Mrs Pinch / It was a house where you could rent a room by the hour, so that a gentleman could lay down and take his mind off business.

Mr Pinch / Unbelievable! What then?

Mrs Pinch / He kissed me a hundred times, and told me he fancied he kissed my pretty sister -meaning me, you know - He said he loved her with all his soul, and told me to be sure to tell her.

Mr Pinch / You stood very still when he kissed you, I hope?

Mrs Pinch / Yes, I swear to you. Would you have wanted me to reveal myself?

Mr Pinch / But you told me he did some beastliness to you. What was it?

Mrs Pinch / Why, he put...

Mr Pinch / Go on.

Mrs Pinch / He put the tip... I told him I'd bite it.

Mr Pinch / The tip of what?

Mrs Pinch / His tongue. And he nuzzled me.

Mr Pinch / Eternal cancer seize his tongue! The dog that he is.

Mrs Pinch / Nay, you need not be so angry with him, for the truth is, he had the sweetest breath.

Mr Pinch / The devil incarnate! You were satisfied with it then, and would do it again?

Mrs Pinch / Not unless he should force me to.

Mr Pinch / Force you? Changeling! I tell you, no woman can be forced.

Mrs Pinch / She may by one such as him, for he's a proper, good strong man. 'Tis hard, let me tell you.

Mr Pinch / What is?

Mrs Pinch / To resist him.

Mr Pinch / (angrily) Go fetch pen, ink, and paper from the next room. Now!

Mrs Pinch / Yes, dear.

[EXIT MRS PINCHWIFE]

Mr Pinch / (aside) Out of Nature's hands they come, plain, open, silly, and fit
for slaves as Heaven intended. But damned love! It is the devil in
them, the passion and lust that leads them astray. I must strangle
that evil monster whilst I can still deal with him.

[RE-ENTER MRS PINCHWIFE WITH PEN AND
PAPER]

Mr Pinch / Come, minx, sit down here and write.

Mrs Pinch / Aye, dearest, but I can't do it very well.

Mr Pinch / I wish you could not at all.

Mrs Pinch / But what should I write?

Mr Pinch / I want you to write a letter to your lover.

Mrs Pinch / Oh Lord, you do tease me, surely you jest.

Mr Pinch / I am not so merry as you think. Come, write as I tell you.

Mrs Pinch / What? Do you think I am a fool?

Mr Pinch / Afraid I will not dictate any words of love to him, dearest? Now,
begin.

Mrs Pinch / Indeed, and indeed, I won't, so I won't.

Mr Pinch / Why not?

Mrs Pinch / Because he's in town, you could send for him if you wanted.

Mr Pinch / You would have him brought to you, is that it? Has it come to
this?
I'm telling you, take up the pen and write or you'll provoke me.
Now, begin. Write; "Sir"

Mrs Pinch / Shouldn't I say, "Dear Sir?" One should always say something more than just "Sir."

Mr Pinch / Write as I tell you, or I'll write whore on your face with this paperknife!

Mrs Pinch / As you say, dearest.
(writes and speaks)

Sir

Mr Pinch / "Though I suffered last night your nauseous, loathsome kisses and embraces"
—Write it down!

Mrs Pinch / No, why should I say that? You know I told you he had sweet breath.

Mr Pinch / Write it!

Mrs Pinch / Let me leave out "loathsome".

Mr Pinch / Write it, I say!

Mrs Pinch / Very well then.

[SHE WRITES]

Mr Pinch / Let me see what have you written.

[HE TAKES THE PAPER AND READS IT OUT LOUD]

Mr Pinch / *Though I suffered last night your kisses and embraces*

- You impudent creature! Where is "nauseous" and "loathsome"?

Mrs Pinch / I can't abide to write such filthy words.

Mr Pinch / Once more write as I tell you, and question it not or I will make sure your pretty little hand never writes again with this!

[HE STABS THE PAPERKNIFE DOWN HARD INTO THE DESKTOP WHERE IT STAYS UPRIGHT THREATENINGLY]

Mrs Pinch / (looking at the knife) Oh Lord! I will.

[SHE WRITES]

Mr Pinch / So let's see now.
[Reads aloud]

Though I suffered last night your nauseous, loathsome kisses and embraces

- Good. Carry on - "yet I would not have you presume that you shall ever repeat them."
- Write it down!

[SHE WRITES]

Mrs Pinch / I have written it.

Mr Pinch / On then. "I must admit to you now, my unfortunate, though innocent frolic, of being in men's clothes."

Mrs Pinch / Done.

Mr Pinch / "May you forevermore cease to pursue her, the one who hates and detests you."

Mrs Pinch / (sighs) Done!

Mr Pinch / Why do you sigh!

Mrs Pinch / I swear, husband, he'll never believe I would write such a letter.

Mr Pinch / What, he'd expect something kinder from you? Come, sign your name only.

Mrs Pinch / Shan't I say "Your most faithful, humble servant till death"?

Mr Pinch / No! Tormenting fiend! Come, fold it now, whilst I go fetch wax and a candle. And write on the backside, "For Mr Horner."

[EXIT MR PINCHWIFE]

Mrs Pinch / (aloud while writing)

For Mr Horner.

[She dots with a flourish]

[SHE DOTS WITH A FLOURISH]

Mrs Pinch / (aside) But why should I send you a letter which will make you angry with me? -Well, I will not send it. -Aye, but then my husband will kill me. -But what do I care what my husband wants? What if I wrote at the bottom my husband made me write it? -Aye, but then my husband would see it.
What should I do? A London woman would have thought of a hundred ideas by now.

[SHE STARES AHEAD DEFEATED, THEN HAS AN IDEA]

Mrs Pinch / Wait - What if I write another letter, and fold it up like this one? Aye, but then my husband would see it.
-Yet by golly I'll try, so I will. I will not send this letter to poor Mr Horner, come what may.

[SHE WRITES AND SPEAKS ALOUD]

Mrs Pinch / (writing)
Dear, sweet Mr Horner – so –

My husband would have me send you a rude, unmannerly letter and would have me say, I hate you. But I won't– so I won't! –

tell a lie for him – so there! –

for I am sure if you and I were in the country together – so –

I could not help treading on your toe under the table and then looking down and blushing - But I must make haste before my husband comes –

(hurried)
And now my husband has taught me to write letters, you shall have longer ones from me, the one who is, dear, dear, Mr Horner, your most humble friend and servant to command till death,

Margery Pinchwife.

Good!

Mrs Pinch / Wait, I must give him a hint at the bottom…

       [SHE WRITES SOMETHING BUT DOES NOT SPEAK
       IT ALOUD]

Mrs Pinch / …like so.
Now fold it up just like the other one – so.
Now write
      For Mr Horner

- But now, what shall I do with it, oh, here comes my husband!

       [RE-ENTER MR PINCHWIFE]

Mr Pinch / I have been detained by that fool of a Count, who pretended he visited me, but I fear he had other motives. Have you finished?

Mrs Pinch / Aye, Aye, dear.

Mr Pinch / Why do you tremble so? Let me see it.

       [HE SNATCHES, OPENS, AND WHILE WE WAIT IN
       SILENCE, HE READS THE LETTER]

Mr Pinch / Come, where's the wax and seal?

Mrs Pinch / Let me see to it, dearest. -Lord, you think me such an absolute fool that I cannot seal a letter. I will do it, so I will.

       [SHE SNATCHES THE LETTER BACK FROM HIM]

Mr Pinch / Very well.

> [SHE EXCHANGES THE LETTER, SEALS IT, AND
> GIVES IT TO HIM]

Mrs Pinch / There. Have I done it correctly?

Mr Pinch / Aye, but I'm certain you would not like it to go now.

Mrs Pinch / Oh, but yes, indeed I would, dear. Right now.

Mr Pinch / Well, you are a good girl then. Come, I will lock you in your
chamber till I come back.

> [EXIT MRS PINCHWIFE. HER HUSBAND LOCKING
> THE DOOR BEHIND HER]

Mr Pinch / (aside) When a man has an attractive wife in a frontier town, he
must protect himself against the treachery and the dogs by
whatever means at his disposal.
And now I've secured her within, I'll deal with the foe without -
with false intelligence.

> [HOLDS UP THE LETTER SMILING. EXITS]

ACT IV SCENE III. MR HORNER'S LODGINGS, LATER THAT DAY

[MR HORNER IS PRESENT]

[DR CRACKER ENTERS]

Dr Cracker / Well, sir, how goes the new plan? Any luck deceiving your friends, or is it finally only yourself you deceive?

Horner / No, good doctor, it is you who is deceived it seems. The dour, surely matrons and the old, rigid husbands think I am as unfit for love as they are. But their wives, sisters, and daughters, well - shall we say - some of them know better already.

Dr Cracker / Already!

Horner / Indeed, even last night I was drunk with half-a-dozen of your 'polite society' as they call themselves. And already I have had the privilege of tying their shoes and garters, warming their night clothes and the like, and - sleeping in their beds, already doctor, already!

Dr Cracker / You have made good use of your time, sir.

Horner / I tell you, I am no more interruption to their lewd behaviour and drunken bawdy songs, than their fat French page who speaks no English.

Dr Cracker / The honourable classes drink and sing bawdy songs?

Horner / Oh, amongst friends, amongst friends. Your hypocrites in honour and religion - they fear the eye of the world more than the eye of Heaven. They have no virtues, yet protest at vice, and live in scandal whilst preaching against sin. Why, I have seen men of the cloth witness the sins of society closets, yet not tell of it in their chapels of confession.

Dr Cracker / Perhaps that is why women these days are more likely to confess their troubles to their priest than their physician.

Horner / Perhaps they are just sick of leeches, doctor.

[KNOCK AT DOOR. SERVANT ENTERS]

Servant / Lady Gooding requests the pleasure of your company, sir.

Horner / Send her in.

[SERVANT EXITS]

Horner / Talking of women of honour, here is an excellent example. Step behind the screen there. See if I do not have particular privileges with the women of reputation already, doctor, already.

[DR CRACKER RETIRES BEHIND A SCREEN AS LADY GOODING ENTERS]

Lady G / Well, Horner, am I not a woman of honour? You can see, I'm as good as my word.

Horner / Indeed, Lady Gooding. And you shall see, madam, in respect of your honour I'll be as good as my word too. Would you care to put me to the test now, madam?

Lady G / First, my dear sir, you must promise to take good care of my dear honour.

Horner / If you utter a word more of your honour, madam, you'll render me incapable of wronging it. There can be no word more deflating to an eager lover.

Lady G / I am astonished, sir. Surely 'honour' from the lips of a lady, has more appeal than 'money' from the mouth of a mistress.

Horner / I am looking forward to finding out, my lady.

Lady G / You can't blame a lady of my reputation for being cautious.

Horner / Cautious! I have been cautious of it already by the story I have created of myself.

Lady G / But you must take great care other women do not know our dear secret, sir. My acquaintances are so critical of others, they would gossip and damage my honour. Oh! 'Tis a wicked, judgmental world, Mr Horner!

Horner / In that case, Lady Gooding, in order to preserve your honour, I'll lie with them all.

Lady G / You'll what?

Horner / It will make the secret their own. That way they'll keep it.

Lady G / Oh no, sir, not like that! A secret is best kept, I hope, by a single person, not by a multitude. I beg you, do not trust anybody else with it, my dear, dear Mr Horner.
-Hold me, let me feel the proof of your honour.

[AS SHE EMBRACES HIM, HER HUSBAND, SIR JASPER GOODING ENTERS]

Sir Jasper / What's going on here!

Lady G / (startled) Oh my husband!
(guiltily) -Sir Jasper, come over here. I am seeing if Mr Horner is ticklish, and he's as ticklish as can be. I love to torment the confounded toad. Let you and I tickle him together.

Sir Jasper / No, your ladyship will tickle him better without me, I suppose. But is this how you buy chinaware? I thought you were going to the china-house.

Horner / China-house! A pox on it! Can you not keep your impertinent wives at home? To be troubled by your own wife is the penalty you pay in marriage, without imposing the troublesome wretches on others. As if keeping her company of an evening was not bad enough without being scarecrow to her vultures by day. At this rate I'll shortly be gentleman dogsbody to the whole town.

Sir Jasper / He! he! he! Poor fellow. Escorting other men's women is like counting other men's money when you can't lay your hands on either. He! he! he!
-Don't be upset, Horner.

Lady G / No, it is I who should be upset, husband. I am left by you to go out indecently alone, or, even worse, left to beg such ill-bred people of your acquaintance as this one, to come with me.

Sir Jasper / Upset? Why, what has he done?

Lady G / Nothing. -Yet.

Sir Jasper / But why do you take offence, if he has done nothing?

Lady G / It is because the unmannerly toad has done nothing, that I am upset.
You see I was resolved he would come with me, for he knows chinaware very well, and has himself a fine collection, but so far I have not succeeded with him.
And will he let me see his own chinaware? No! Not unless I beg and beg him till he is fed up with me. But I will find it, and have what I came for yet.

Horner / Madam, I will never tell you which room to find it, lest you lock yourself in for hours enjoying it, and wonder why you have nothing like it at home.

Lady G / (interested) For hours?

[SHE RUSHES FOR THE BEDCHAMBER, ENTERING AND LOCKING THE DOOR BEHIND HER]

Horner / [rattling the door handle]   So, she has got into my bedchamber and locked me out.
Oh the impertinency of woman-kind! Sir Jasper, if you ever allow your insufferable wife to trouble me here again, I shall make sure she is unable to sit down for a week, by my lord mayor I shall!
-Though the days of doing such things for pleasure are now sadly passed for me.

Sir Jasper / Ha! ha! he! At my first coming in, I was half jealous, but now I see my folly. He! he! he! Poor Horner.

Horner / You may laugh now, but it will be my turn before long. Oh women! More impertinent, more cunning, and more mischievous than a barrel of monkeys, and to me almost as ugly!

[THE SOUND OF ITEMS BEING THROWN AND
MOVED ABOUT IS HEARD]

Horner / And now she throws my things about and rifles through all I
have. But I'll get in to her the back way and give her what for,
see if I don't!

Sir Jasper / Ha! ha! ha! Poor angry, Horner.

Horner / Wait here, I'll ferret her out. And when I'm done with her you can
take her with you.

[HORNER EXITS AT THE OTHER DOOR]
[SIR JASPER TALKS THROUGH THE DOOR TO HIS
WIFE]

Sir Jasper / Darling wife! My Lady Gooding! He is coming in to you the
back way.

Lady G / (within) Let him come, which ever way he will. I am more than
ready for him.

Sir Jasper / He'll catch you, and use you roughly, and be too strong for you.

Lady G / Don't you trouble yourself, let him if he is man enough.

Horner / (within sternly) Lady Gooding!

Lady G / (squeals) Oh Mr Horner! How big you look when you come at
me! I hope you are not going to spare me the rod. After all, I have
been a very naughty girl.

[THE SOUNDS OF EXERTION AND SURPRISE ARE
HEARD AS IF A STRUGGLE IS TAKING PLACE
WITHIN. INTERMITTANT GIGGLES AND
LAUGHTER QUIETENING DOWN TO
OCCASIONAL EXCLAMATIONS THROUGHOUT
THE FOLLOWING]

Sir Jasper / (through door) Are your intentions honourable or dishonourable,
Mr Horner? He! He! he!

Horner /   (within struggling) I didn't realize I had a choice.

Sir Jasper /   You don't! He! He! Not anymore. Ha! Ha! Ha!
Give her what for, Horner! She deserves it, the minx.

Lady G /   (giggles within) Oh Mr Horner! You are so masterful. My
husband would never think of using the back way to come at me.

Dr Cracker /   [aside]. If I had not seen this with my own eyes, I would never
have believed it!

[ANITA QUIM KNOCKS AT THE FRONT DOOR]

Anita Quim /   (off loud) Where's this woman-hater, this toad, this ugly, greasy,
dirty sloven?

Sir Jasper /   [aside]. So, the women all think him ugly now, eh? It seems his
lacking makes him repugnant to them. As my wife said
yesterday; a eunuch is never handsome to a woman, in the same
way a rich man is never ugly.

[ENTER A DETERMINED ANITA QUIM]

Anita Quim /   (surprised) Oh! Sir Jasper.
-Where is that odious beast, Horner?

Sir Jasper /   He's in his chamber, with my wife. She's teasing him.

Anita Quim /   Is she now? And he's the clownish beast who'll give her no
quarter by teasing her back, I suppose. I must go help her.
[tries the door]
What, the door's locked?

Sir Jasper /   Aye, my wife locked it.

Anita Quim /   Did she now? I'll break it open then.

Sir Jasper /   No, no, no. He'll do her no harm.

Anita Quim /   Is there no other way to get in to them? Where does this go?
I'll disturb them all right.

[SHE EXITS AT ANOTHER DOOR]

[MORE KNOCKING ON FRONT DOOR - ENTER OLD LADY QUIM]

Lady Quim / (off) Where is the harlot, the impudent baggage, the rambling tomrigg?

Sir Jasper / (aside) He serves a lot of women, it seems.

[ENTER OLD LADY QUIM]

Lady Quim / Oh, Sir Jasper, I'm glad to see you here. Did you not see my vile grand-daughter come in here just now?

Sir Jasper / Yes I did, Lady Quim.

Lady Quim / Well, where is she then? Where is she? Lord, I have rattled myself to pieces in pursuit of her. And why does she come here? Which woman lodges here?

Sir Jasper / None.

Lady Quim / None? If this is not a woman's lodgings, why does she come here then? Are you sure no woman lodges here?

Sir Jasper / No, nor any man for that matter. This is Mr Horner's lodgings.

Lady Quim / Is it now. Are you sure?

Sir Jasper / Quite sure.

Lady Quim / So! Then there's no harm in it, I hope. But where is he?

Sir Jasper / He's in the next room with my wife.

Lady Quim / Well, if you trust him with your wife, then I suppose I may with my Biddy.

[A COUPLE OF SQUEALS OF DELIGHT ARE HEARD WITHIN]

[OLD LADY QUIM PAUSES FOR A MOMENT THEN CARRIES ON]

Lady Quim / They say he's a harmless man now, as harmless as any man that ever came out of Italy with a good voice.

Sir Jasper / Aye, aye. Poor man.

[RE-ENTER YOUNG ANITA QUIM]

Anita Quim / I can't find them.

Lady Quim / Find whom?

Anita Quim / (taken by surprise) Oh! Grandmother. What are you doing here?

Lady Quim / Never mind what I am doing here, strumpet, what are you doing in a gentleman's lodgings?

Anita Quim / (regaining composure, guiltily)
I, um, followed Lady Gooding here, grandmother. 'Tis the prettiest lodgings, and I have been looking at the prettiest of pictures. But I couldn't find the ones I was looking for.

[RE-ENTER LADY GOODING WITH A PIECE OF CHINA IN HER HAND, AND HORNER FOLLOWING. THEY LOOK RUFFLED AND FLUSHED]

Lady G / Oh! Anita Quim. (accusingly) I didn't expect to see you here. -Dearest husband, I have been toiling and moiling for the prettiest piece of china.

Horner / Indeed, she has been hard work for me, I did what I could.

Anita Quim / Oh, lord, I'll have some china too, good Mr Horner. Don't think you can give other people your china and me none. Come in with me too.

Horner / Upon my honour, I have none left now.

Anita Quim / Nay, nay, I have known you deny your china before now, but you shan't put me off, so come.

Horner / This lady had the last there was.

Lady G / Yes indeed, madam, to my certain knowledge, he has no more china.

Anita Quim / Oh, but it may be he has some left for me.

Lady G / What? Do you think if he had had any left I would not have had it too? We women of quality take it all, we can never get enough china.

Horner / Do not take it badly, I will have china for you another time.

Anita Quim / Thank you, dear toad.

Lady G / (hissed aside to Horner) And what do you mean by that promise, Horner?

Horner / (aside to Gooding) Poor thing, she has only an innocent, literal understanding of china.

Lady Quim / Poor Mr Horner! He has more than his hands full pleasing you all, I see.

Horner / Aye, madam, you see how they use me!

Lady Quim / Poor gentleman, I pity you.

Horner / I thank you, madam. I need pity from such reverend ladies as yourself, the young ones will never allow a man a moment's rest.

Anita Quim / Come, beast, and dine with us. We shall need a man at cards after dinner, and later I have something that will require the aid of a strong man.

Horner / That's all their use is of me, madam, as you can see.

Anita Quim / Come, sloven, I'll lead you like the dog that your are, to be sure of you getting there.

[SHE PULLS HIM BY THE CRAVAT]

Lady Quim / Alas, poor man, how she tugs him! Smack her. Go on, give her a good spanking, man. That's the way to make well bred women quiet.

Horner / No, madam, I fear that would just make her want to torment me more.

Anita Quim / Foh, you filthy toad! Now I've done with jesting.

Lady Quim / Go on, spank her, do it for me. It used to work for me when I was wayward.

Horner / Well, for you madam, how could I refuse. I will spank her but do not expect me to kiss her better afterwards.

[HORNER SPANKS ANITA QUIM PLAYFULLY ON THE BEHIND]

Anita Quim / (squeals) You will pay dearly for this later, Horner!

Lady Quim / Ha! ha! ha! I told you so, and now for the kiss.

Anita Quim / Foh! a kiss of his?

Sir Jasper / Has no more harm in it than one of my spaniel's. ha ha.

Lady Quim / And no more good either. He! He!

Dr Cracker / (aside from behind screen) I will now believe anything he tells me.

[MR PINCHWIFE KNOCKS AND ENTERS THE FRONT DOOR]

Pinchwife / (distant loud voice) Where is the confounded man?

Lady G / Oh lord, there's a man at the door, husband! Come, I should not be seen here.

Sir Jasper / Not even when I am with you, dearest?

Lady G /   No, no, think of my honour. Let's be gone.

Anita Quim /   Grandmother, quickly, out the back way. Goodness knows what he would say or think of us as well.

Lady G /   To be found in the lodgings of anything like a man! - Quick, away.

[EXEUNT SIR JASPER, LADY GOODING, OLD LADY QUIM, AND ANITA QUIM]

Lady Quim /   (disappearing into distance) How did you know there was a back way?

Anita Quim /   (off) Oh grandmother. Stop being so old fashioned. The back entrance is used like the front entrance these days. It's not just the servants who enjoy its use anymore.

[ENTER MR PINCHWIFE]

Horner /   Pinchwife. Well, what brings you here, my dear friend?

Mr Pinch /   Your impertinence.

Horner /   My impertinence? Why, you gentlemen with pretty little wives think you have the privilege of saying anything you like to your friends, and are as brutish about it as our creditors.

Mr Pinch /   Sir, I will never trust you in any way.

Horner /   Why mistrust me? You know me so well.

Mr Pinch /   Because I know you so well.

Horner /   Haven't I always been your friend? 'Honest Jack'? Why be so off with me? Come, kiss me, dear rogue. Gad, I always was, and always will be your servant

Mr Pinch /   So, you wish to send another kiss to my wife, is that it?

Horner /   So, there it is. A man can't show his friendship to a married man,
without him talking about his wife to you. Please I beg you, leave
your wife out of this, and let you and I be friends again as we
were before. Why, you treat me with the contempt of one who
was about to rob you.

Mr Pinch /   You are being over-kind and civil to me as if I were your cuckold
already. And so you should, sir, since I am so kind and civil to
you as to bring you this.
Here, sir.

[MR PINCHWIFE HANDS MR HORNER THE
LETTER]

Horner /   What is this?

Mr Pinch /   Only a love letter, sir.

Horner /   From whom?
[opens letter, skims]
Why! This is from your wife.

Mr Pinch /   Yes, from my wife, sir. Am I not wonderfully kind and civil to
you now? Though you'll not think so of her.

Horner /   [reads] - hmm- and hmm.
Ha! Is this a trick of yours or hers?

Mr Pinch /   The gentleman is surprised I find. – What's the matter? You
expected a kinder letter?

Horner /   No indeed, how could I?

Mr Pinch /   Yes, yes, I'm sure you did. A man of your reputation must be
disappointed if the women do not declare their passion and fall at
your feet at the first opportunity.

Horner / Your imagination surpasses you, sir? Wait…
-(reads aside to self)

P.S. Be sure I love you, whatever my husband says, and don't let him see this, lest he should come home and punch me, or kill my squirrel."

Mr Pinch / Come, don't think about it so much.

Horner / I can't help it.

Mr Pinch / Does the letter not warrant a comment? I bring you a letter from my wife, and let you kiss and court her to my face.

Horner / You are mad with jealousy. I never saw your wife in my life before the play the other day, and I had no way of knowing then if it was her or not. I courted her and kissed her?

Mr Pinch / I say again, you kissed and courted my wife last night, in men's clothes, as she confesses in her letter…

Horner / That was your wife! Why didn't you tell me it was her? Indeed, my freedom with her was your fault, not mine.

Mr Pinch / So, it was, was it?

Horner / Fy! I'd never do it to a woman before her husband's face, for sure.

Mr Pinch / No? Well I would rather you do it to my wife before my face than behind my back.

Horner / No. You would put me off.

Mr Pinch / (angry) I would put you off all right, and you can see by her letter she would too!
I will not be a cuckold, I tell you, there will be danger in making me a cuckold.

Horner / Why? Were you not well cured of your last dose of the clap?

Mr Pinch / (angry) I carry a knife, sir.

Horner / And it should be taken from you in case you do yourself a mischief. You are a madman.

Mr Pinch / Well sir, madman or not, I will have my answer before we part. Or do I have to do 'yourself' a mischief? I assure you, sir, it was written voluntarily. I had no hand in it, you can believe me.

Horner / Indeed, I do believe you.

Mr Pinch / And believe her too, she's an innocent creature with nothing to hide, sir.

Horner / Pray, Mr Pinchwife, present my humble greetings to her, and tell her, I will obey her letter to the letter, and fulfil her desires whatever they may be, or however difficult they are to achieve. Then you shall no longer have need to protect her, I assure her, and you.

Mr Pinch / Well then, farewell. And play with any man's honour but mine, kiss any man's wife but mine, you're welcome to them.

[MR PINCHWIFE EXITS. DOCTOR REMERGES FROM HIDING]

Horner / Ha! ha! ha! doctor. Did you hear all that?

Dr Cracker / It seems it is him that has not heard, the news about you at least, or he chooses not to believe it.

Horner / Ha! ha! -now, doctor, what do you think?

Dr Cracker / Pray, let me see the letter.
                  [opens letter and reads]
                  -hmm- "for - dear - love you-"

Horner / I wonder how she contrived it! What do you think? It's original at least.

Dr Cracker / Like your cuckolds. They are not like common cuckolds. I now believe it possible that you could cuckold the Grand Sultan himself, even with his guard of eunuchs.

Horner / Well, doctor. The poor woman has stretched forth her hand and called out for help. What can a gentleman do but help a lady find satisfaction in her hour of need?

Dr Cracker / I am speechless. Quite speechless.

Horner / Ha! Ha! Well, I am headed for my club. I am in need of sustenance. One must keep one's strength up!

Act IV Scene IV. A Gentleman's Club In Town

[HORNER IS SEATED IN HIS CLUB AFTER A
HEARTY MEAL]

[THE DOOR OPENS AND PINCHWIFE PEERS ROUND
THE DOOR. SPYING HORNER HE EXITS AGAIN.
MOMENTS LATER THE DOOR RE-OPENS AND
SPARKISH ENTERS, PULLING IN A PROTESTING MR
PINCHWIFE BY THE ARM]

Sparkish / (entering) Come back here, Mr Pinchwife! What a good brother-in-
law you are! Neither going to church nor to dinner with your newly
wed sister!

Mr Pinch / (dragged) My sister denies her marriage, and as you can see has left
you dissatisfied.

Sparkish / Pshaw! Only on the minor point that our parson was not legally
qualified.
But it's only her first day modesty I believe. She'll come to her
senses by nightfall, and I shall have my fill of her senses then.
-In the meantime, you and Harry Horner (looks around) – ah good
he is here - must dine with me.
(drags Pinchwife to Horner) My wedding feast awaits at my aunt's
in the Piazza.

Horner / Your wedding! What stale maid has lived to be so desperate for a
husband?

Sparkish / If you please, sir, it is this gentleman's sister you refer too, - and
she's no stale maid.

Horner / I'm sorry to hear that.

Sparkish / Sorry? Sorry for what? Have you heard any ill of her?

Horner / No, no, sorry for her sake, not yours, and another man's sake that
had hopes, I thought.

Sparkish / Another man! Another man! What is his name?

Horner / Nay, since it's in the past, he shall remain nameless.
Poor Hancock. He'll be sorry he missed it.

Mr Pinch / I doubt that. He seemed to be much troubled by the match.
Anyway, I must take my leave now.

Sparkish / No, you shan't go, brother.

Mr Pinch / Of necessity I must, but I will come to you later for dinner.

[MR PINCHWIFE EXITS HURRIEDLY]

Sparkish / (gestures rudely after Pinchwife) Pah!
But, Harry, what did you mean? Have I a rival in my wife already?
But come to think of it, he may be of use to me later. Though I can
now fall heartily on my wife without the need to spice up my
ardour, there will come a time when a rival will be as good a spice
to a wife, as gooseberry sauce is to a goose.

Horner / Oh you damned rogue! You have set my teeth on edge with your
gooseberry.

Sparkish / Then let's go to dinner.
I am supposed to be taking you there, my wife will be waiting.
Come along, quickly.

Horner / Who is dining with you?

Sparkish / My friends and relations, my brother Pinchwife, so there will be
one of your acquaintances there at least.

Horner / And his pretty wife?

Sparkish / 'Gad no, he'll not let her come amongst us good fellows. The
cunning countryman keeps his wife like he keeps his little firkin of
ale - for his own drinking - and a gentleman can't get a sniff of it.
'Gad, I am witty I think, considering I was married to-day...
- By the world! quickly, come.

Horner / I have just dined, so I see no point in dining with you, unless you
fetch her too.

Sparkish / Pshaw! What pleasure can you have with women now, Harry?

Horner / My eyes are not gone. And besides her husband is a frightful bore and ugly with it. His wife is far more interesting and pleasant on the eye.

Sparkish / There's still embers in the hearth, but the fire has gone out, is that it? He! He!

Horner / I still love a good prospect, and I will not dine with you unless she does too. Go fetch her, but do not tell her husband it is for my sake.

Sparkish / Well, for your sake I'll try. Meet me at my aunt's lodgings in an hour.

Horner / I wouldn't miss it for the world.

ACT IV SCENE V. MR PINCHWIFE'S LODGINGS

[MRS PINCHWIFE IS LEANING ON HER ELBOW AT
A TABLE WRITING]

Mrs Pinch / (aside) So, it has happened. I have the London disease. I am sick
of my husband, and sick for my admirer. When I think of my
husband, I tremble in a cold sweat and feel nauseous, and when I
think of my dear, dear Mr Horner, I am all of a fever and delirious.
But then I dream of being removed from my bedchamber to his,
and I am suddenly well again, indeed and indeed.

Ah, poor Mr Horner! Well, I cannot – no, I will not - stay here.
Therefore I shall end my letter to him, which shall be a finer letter
than my last because I have studied it like anything. Oh sick, sick
again!

[SHE TAKES HER PEN AND WRITES]

[ENTER PINCHWIFE, WHO SEEING HER WRITING,
STEALS SOFTLY BEHIND HER AND LOOKING
OVER HER SHOULDER, SNATCHES THE PAPER
FROM HER]

Mr Pinch / Writing more letters?

Mrs Pinch / (startled) Oh Lord, dearest! Why do you frighten me so?

Mr Pinch / What's this?

[SHE TRIES TO RUN OUT. HE STOPS HER, AND
READS]

Mr Pinch / [forcefully restraining her] Nay, you shall not leave, madam
[reads aloud]
"Dear, dear, dear Mr Horner"

My teaching you to write letters has been put to good purpose I
see. Let's read the rest of it shall we?

"First, I must beg your pardon for my boldness in writing to you, which I would not have done had you not said first you loved me so extremely. If you truly, truly do, you would not want to see me suffer by lying in the arms of another man whom I loathe and detest to the point of sickness."

-Now you can write these filthy words I see. What else-

"Therefore, I hope you will speedily find some way to free me from this unfortunate match, which was never, I assure you, of my choosing. However, if you love me, as I do you, you must help me away before tomorrow, or else, alas! I shall be for ever out of your reach. I can defer no longer our..."

- Our? What was to follow 'our'? – 'Our' journey into the country I suppose?
Damn woman! -Now put an end to your letter, or I'll put an end to you, with all my plagues at once!

[HOLDS HIS CANE ABOVE HER HEAD AS IF TO CANE HER]

Mrs Pinch / Oh Lord, don't be so angry with me, dearest!

[ENTER COUNT SPARKISH]

Sparkish / Well now, what's going on here?

Mr Pinch / This fool here is!

[MRS PINCHWIFE SOBS AND COVERS HER FACE]

Sparkish / What? Brandishing your cane at your wife? You should never do that, except at night in the dark when no one can see. It can be fun, so I have heard tell.

Mr Pinch / What a man does with his own wife in his own home is no business of any other man, especially a man as insensible and open as yourself.

Sparkish / Come, come, you are my family now, and as such you and your wife must dine with me. Dinner's ready, come along.
-But where is my wife? Has she not come home yet? Where is she?

Mr Pinch / Making you a cuckold. It's what they all do, as soon as they can.

Sparkish / What, on our wedding-day? No, no. I am sure a wife will at least let her husband have first bite of the apple of love on her wedding day, by the world.
But come, they are awaiting us at dinner. Come, come, I'll lead down our Margery.

Mr Pinch / No! –sir. Go, we'll follow you.

Sparkish / I will not leave without you.

Mr Pinch / By the world, you are becoming irritating, sir.

Sparkish / Come, come, Madam Margery.

Mr Pinch / Do not attempt to treat your friends with my wife, because you have lost your own!
-I'll take her myself.

Sparkish / Lord, you are so shy of your wife! I said this would happen.

Mr Pinch / Said what would happen?

Sparkish / Let me tell you, brother, we men of wit have a saying; cuckolding is like the pox. The danger of infection is always present. You may try hiding them away, but if women's minds incline them to stray, no power in the world will stop them.

Mr Pinch / What kind of fool allows himself to be a cuckold, a thing of ridicule!
Well, sir, since you are so aware of the danger, let me advise you not to neglect your own wife. Remember;
"However a wife's belly comes to swell,
The husband's the one that pays for it all".
Now go on ahead. I will follow.

Sparkish / Very well, but don't be taking too long or I will be upset.

[EXIT SPARKISH]

Mr Pinch / Come on, take the pen and put the ending to the letter you intended. If you are false even in a single letter, I will know, and punish you severely.

[BRANDISHES HIS CANE]

Mr Pinch / What was to follow -let's see now –

"you must help me away before tomorrow, or else, alas! I shall be for ever out of your reach. I can defer no longer our..."

-What follows "our"?

Mrs Pinch / Must it all come out, then, dear?

Mr Pinch / Yes! Write!

Mrs Pinch / As you say dearest.

[MRS PINCHWIFE TAKES THE PEN AND WRITES]

Mr Pinch / Let's see-
[reads as she writes]

"For I can defer no longer our... wedding..."

Wedding!

"Your... slighted... Alithea."

'Alithea'? What's the meaning of this? My sister's name on it?!

Mrs Pinch / Yes, indeed, dearest.

Mr Pinch / But why her name on it? Speak! Tell me, I say!

Mrs Pinch / Aye, But you'll tell her then.
(She pauses, then looks him straight in the face)
    If I could trust you not to tell her…

Mr Pinch / I don't know what to think anymore. I am stunned, my head is
spinning. Explain!

Mrs Pinch / You won't tell her, indeed, and indeed?

Mr Pinch / No! Tell me.

Mrs Pinch / She'll be angry with me. But I'd rather she were angry with me
than you, dear.
It was her that made me write the letter, and taught me what I
should write.

Mr Pinch / Ha! I suspected the style was somewhat better than your own.
But why would she make you write to him when she can write a
letter herself?

Mrs Pinch / Why, she said because…
-I was unwilling to do it for her at first. (pauses as if finished)

Mr Pinch / Because what? Because?

Mrs Pinch / Oh... because... in case Mr Horner should be cruel and refuse her, or afterwards show the letter around, she could disown it. The handwriting not being hers after all.

Mr Pinch / Really? Ha! Then I think I should calm myself down. You, my little changeling could not invent a lie like this.
   -But wait, what if you could. But why would you? You know I would find out.
   -Wait - Now I think about it, Horner said he was sorry she had married the Count, and she disowned her marriage earlier, perhaps that was for Horner's sake..
   -But listen here, madam. Your sister went out in the morning, and I have not seen her here since.

Mrs Pinch / Alack-a-day, she has been crying all day upstairs it seems, huddled in a corner.

Mr Pinch / Where is she? Let me speak with her.

Mrs Pinch / Oh Lord, do you mean to have me found out? She'll know I've told you then. Please, dearest, let me talk with her first.

Mr Pinch / I must speak with her to know whether Horner ever made her any promises, and if she is married to the Count or not.

Mrs Pinch / Please, dear husband, don't. Not till I have spoken with her. She'll kill me otherwise.

Mr Pinch / Go on then, and tell her to come out to me.

Mrs Pinch / Yes, yes, dear.

[MRS PINCHWIFE HURRIEDLY RUNS OUT]

Mr Pinch / (aside waiting for his wife) Well, that settles it, Horner can have her. I'd rather give him my sister than lend him my wife. And such an alliance will prevent his pretensions to my wife, for sure. I'll make him kin to her, then he won't care for her.

[RE-ENTER MRS PINCHWIFE]

Mrs Pinch / Oh Lord, husband! I told you it would make my sister angry.

Mr Pinch / Won't she come down?

Mrs Pinch / No, dear. She's ashamed to look you in the face. And she says, if you go in to her, she'll run away downstairs, and in her shame go straight to Mr Horner, whom she says has promised her marriage.

Mr Pinch / Did he now? Promise her marriage? Then marriage she shall have. If she would be so good as to come down and discuss it with me, I will set about arranging it immediately. Go. Go tell her so.

[EXIT MRS PINCHWIFE]

Mr Pinch / (aside) His estate is equal to the Count's, and his intellect is by far the better, -and I'd rather be known as his brother-in-law, than his cuckold.

[RE-ENTER MRS PINCHWIFE]

Mr Pinch / Well? What does she say now?

Mrs Pinch / She says, she would only have you lead her to Horner's lodgings - with whom she will first discuss the matter before she talks with you, which she cannot do for alas, poor creature, she says she cannot so much as look you in the face.

Mr Pinch / Tell her to come down.

Mrs Pinch / She says she will only come to you in a mask, and if you will not lecture her or question her, she'll come down to you immediately.

Mr Pinch / Tell her I'll not speak a word to her, or require a word from her.

Mrs Pinch / Oh, I forgot. She says she cannot look you in the face, even through a mask. Therefore she asks that you put out the candle.

Mr Pinch / I agree, I agree tell her. And tell her to make haste.
            [blows out candle]
              -There, the candle is out.-

[EXIT MRS PINCHWIFE AND THE CANDLE IS PUT OUT]

Mr Pinch /   (aside) I'll have to take her to Horner and confront him with all this. Still, I am glad it is my sister he wants now and not my wife. I seem to have as much trouble getting people to lie with my sister as I do stopping them lying with my wife.
Where have they got to?

> [RE-ENTER MRS PINCHWIFE MASKED WITH HOOD AND SCARFS AND A NIGHT-GOWN AND PETTICOAT OF ALITHEA'S]

Mr Pinch /   Is that you, sister? Let us go then. But first, let me lock up my wife.
-Margery, where are you?

Mrs Pinch /   Here, dearest.

Mr Pinch /   Come here so that I may lock you up in your room.

Mrs Pinch /   Yes, dear.

> [SHE TAKES HIS HAND AS HE GUIDES HER IN THE ROOM. WHEN HE LETS HER GO SHE STEALS SOFTLY TO THE OTHER SIDE OF HIM AS HE LOCKS THE DOOR. SHE TAKES HIS OTHER HAND AND IS LED AWAY AS ALITHEA]

Mr Pinch /   Come, sister, where are you now?
(taking her hand)
Good. Let us go.

End of Act IV

ACT V

ACT V SCENE I. MR HORNER'S LODGINGS

[HORNER IS PRESENT, DR CRACKER COMES INTO THE ROOM]

Dr Cracker / What, all alone, Horner? Not so much as one of your cuckolds here, or one of their wives? They seem to appear together these days.

Horner / That's the irony of it. A cuckold tends to keep his eye firmly on his wife, and so finds himself more in her company than he ever would if she were faithful. It even hinders his own pleasures.

Dr Cracker / So his company wearies you almost as soon as hers, I suppose.

Horner / A pox it does! Keeping a cuckold company after you have had his wife is tiresome. And you know what women are like when you have just had them, you can't be rid of them. The only way is to upset them with a scathing comment.

Dr Cracker / I see. So at first a man makes a friend of the husband to get to the wife, then has to fall out with the wife to be rid of the husband.

Horner / Just like bankers, once a man has lost his credit to us, we can't bear his company again.

Dr Cracker / And just like bankers, at first to draw him in, you are overly kind and dear, -as you were to Pinchwife. But what became of that intrigue with his wife?

Horner / A pox on it! He's as uncivil as a man who's already been cheated. And since he's so protective, his wife's attentions are in vain. She is so very young and beautiful though, with such an appealing innocence.

Dr Cracker / But she sent you a letter by him.

Horner / Yes, and that's a riddle I have not yet solved. Allowing the poor creature to offer herself, and yet he keeps so close a guard on her.

Dr Cracker / Hmm, so close he makes her more the willing, and that of course adds the additional element of revenge to her desire.

Horner / Quite. Willing and revenge: happy bedfellows which lead to a happy bedfellow in my book.

[KNOCKS AT THE DOOR. ENTER SERVANT]

Servant / Mr Pinchwife is here to see you, sir, with a lady.

Horner / What! Talk of the devil. Here's just the man now. Send him in.

Dr Cracker / This should prove interesting.

[ENTER PINCHWIFE, LEADING IN HIS WIFE MASKED, MUFFLED, AND IN HER SISTER'S GOWN]

Horner / What is the meaning of this, Pinchwife?

Mr Pinch / The last time, as you know, sir, I brought you a love-letter. Now, I bring you a mistress. I think you'll say I am a civil man to you.

Horner / The devil take me! I would say you are the most civil man I ever met, and I have known some. This is better than bringing me letters. But, listen, a word in your ear
-(aside to Pinchwife) Just the usual question. Is she sound? On your word?

Mr Pinch / What do you take us for? A wench and her pimp?!

Horner / Pshaw! Wench and pimp, just words. I know you are an honest fellow and have great acquaintance among the ladies. Have you perhaps found a love for me there, to keep me from making love to your wife?

Mr Pinch / Sir, I am not one for fooling.

Horner / Nor I. Therefore I pray, let us see her face. Are you sure I don't know her?

Mr Pinch / I am sure you do know her.

Horner / A pox! Why do you bring her to me then?

Mr Pinch / Because she's a relation of mine.

Horner / Is she indeed? Then you are even more civil and obliging than I thought, you old rogue.

Mr Pinch / She desired me to bring her to you.

Horner / Then she is obliging too.

Mr Pinch / You'll make her welcome for my sake, I hope.

Horner / For your sake? I hope she is willing enough to make her own welcome. Now unmask her.

Mr Pinch / You speak to her. She doesn't listen to me.

Horner / Madam-
      [Mrs Pinchwife signals to shush and get rid of Pinchwife]
        She wishes to speak with me in private. Please wait outside, sir.

Mr Pinch / She's unwilling to talk in front of me. By rights I should know all her indecent conduct in this whole sordid business, but, I'll leave you together and hope when I am gone, you'll agree. If not, you and I shan't agree, sir.

Horner / Whether she and I agree or not has no standing between you and I.

      [MRS PINCHWIFE MAKES SIGNS WITH HER HAND FOR HIM TO BE GONE]

Horner / She bids you leave, sir.

Mr Pinch / (leaving) In the meantime I'll fetch a parson, and I'd better find Count Sparkish to inform him, now I am rid of her, and all the trouble she causes me.

[PINCHWIFE EXITS AS HORNER AND DR
CRACKER LOOK ON IN BEMUSEMENT]

[THE SERVANT ENTERS AGAIN]

Servant / Sir Jasper Gooding is here, sir.

Horner / A pox on him! What does he want with me? All right send him
up.

[EXIT SERVANT]

Horner / This is the trouble with a cuckold we were talking of, doctor.
Does he not have enough to do hindering his wife's sport without
hindering other women's too?
　(beckoning to Mrs Pinchwife)　　-Step in here, madam. I'll
be right with you.

[EXIT MRS PINCHWIFE THROUGH ONE DOOR]
[ENTER SIR JASPER GOODING THROUGH
ANOTHER]

Sir Jasper / Horner. My best and dearest friend.

Horner / (aside to Dr Cracker) See, the classic approach, doctor.

Dr Cracker / Indeed, indeed.

Horner / Well, be brief, Sir. Jasper, I am busy. What would your
impertinent wife want now?

Sir Jasper / Well guessed, indeed. I do come from her.

Horner / To invite me to supper? Tell her, I can't come. Now leave.

Sir Jasper / Nay, now you are wrong. My lady, and the whole knot of the
'virtuous gang' - as they call themselves - are resolved upon a
frolic of coming to you tonight for a ball in masquerade, and are
all dressed up in readiness.

Horner / I shan't be at home.

Sir Jasper / Lord, how uncivil you are to women now! Nay, I beg you, please don't disappoint them. They'll think it my fault. I'll arrange the banquet and the fiddles. But say nothing about it to anyone. The poor virtuous scallywags would not have it known for the world that they go masquerading, and they say they are interested in no man's balls but yours.

Horner / Good grief. Well, be gone. And tell them from me, if they come it will be at the peril of their honour and yours.

Sir Jasper / He! he! he! We'll hold you to that. Farewell.

[EXIT SIR JASPER]

Horner / Doctor, you too shall be my guest. But now I have to a private feast to attend.

[HORNER ENTERS THE CHAMBER WITH AN EAGER SMILE, RUBBING HIS HANDS TOGETHER]

ACT V SCENE II. THE PIAZZA OF COVENT GARDEN

[SPARKISH WALKS WITH A LETTER IN HIS HAND,
PINCHWIFE FOLLOWING]

Sparkish / (brandishing letter in anger) But who would have thought a
woman could have been so false to me? By the world, I would not
have thought it.

Mr Pinch / You were all for giving and taking liberties. She has seen fit to
take it, sir, as you can see in that letter. You are an open person, so
is she, as you can see there.

Sparkish / Well, if this is her handwriting, I've not seen it before.

Mr Pinch / Whether it is or not, it was this hand which led her to Mr Horner. I
left her there just now to fetch a parson at their request. It seems
yours was just a mock marriage.

Sparkish / Indeed, she insists it was Hancock in a parson's habit who married
us. But I'm sure he told me it was his brother, Ned.

Mr Pinch / Oh, there it's out, you were deceived, not her, for you are such an open person. But I must be gone. -You'll find her at Mr Horner's. Go, and believe your own eyes.

[EXIT PINCHWIFE]

Sparkish / (aside) I'll go to her all right, the shameless hussy! -But wait, was she not out walking earlier? At the other end of the Piazza from Horner's?   - I'm sure she was.

[ENTER ALITHEA AND LUCY, WALKING]

Sparkish / Alithea! It is good meeting with you, madam, though I doubt you'd think so.
I hear you made a short visit to Mr Horner. And I suppose you'll be returning to him presently, ready for the parson when he arrives.

Alithea / Mr Horner and a parson?

Sparkish / Come, madam, no more pretence, no more jilting. I am no longer a generous person.

Alithea / What's this?

Lucy / (aside sarcastically) This marriage is going to work, I see.

Sparkish / Could you find no easy country fool to abuse? No one but me? A gentleman of wit and pleasure about the town? Was it your pride that decided you were too good for an intellectual man? Unworthy, deceitful woman! As false as the dice on a tricksters stall.

Lucy / By his confused babbling he's been at the bubble, I'd say. And gambling,

Alithea / He has been overdoing the merriment at his wedding-dinner, that's for sure.

Sparkish / What? As if that is not enough, you mock me too?

Alithea / I have no idea what you are talking about.

Sparkish / Your bare-faced effrontery amazes me madam. Do you pretend
not to have written an impudent letter to Mr Horner? Who I now
realise has clubbed with you in deluding me with his pretence of
an aversion to women, so I might not, indeed, suspect.

Alithea / I wrote a letter to Mr Horner?

Sparkish / Do not deny it, madam. Your brother showed it to me just now,
and told me how he had left you at Horner's lodgings to fetch a
parson to marry you. I wish you joy, madam, joy, joyous joy. And
to him too, much joy. And to myself more joy, for not marrying
you!

Alithea / My brother broke off the match? And I consented to it?
(to Lucy) It seems this gentleman can be made jealous after all,
Lucy! He speaks to me as if I were his wife. Perhaps it was a real
parson who married us after all.

Sparkish / I suppose that was a contrivance of Horner's and yours to make
Hancock play the parson. Not that I would want him to be a real
parson any more than you now, no, not for the world.
-And shall I tell you another truth? I never had any passion for you
till now, for now I hate you. It's true. I was marrying you for your
dowry as other intellectual men around town do, and to show you
how unconcerned I am, I'll come to your wedding, and wish you as
much joy as I would a stale wench plucked out of the gutter. And
what's more, with as much - or rather as little - joy as I would
have felt on our first night if I had married you.
There! That told you. And so, I bid you good day.

[HE EXITS LEAVING HER SPEECHLESS]

Alithea / (to Lucy) How was I ever so deceived in a man!

Lucy / You believe the fool can be made jealous now?

Alithea / But so weak in character.

Lucy / A weakness which allowed him to be led into marriage by a future
wife (looks sternly at Alithea) -who did not love him- and which
now allows him to be persuaded against it by that idiot brother of
yours.

Alithea / But marry Mr Horner! My brother does not intend it, surely? If I thought he did, I would take your advice and marry Mr Hancock in an instant.
If there is any other woman stupid enough to marry that foolish Count for fortune and title, she deserves all she gets.

Lucy / Madam, she would need to be stupid to marry him, and may he deserve her.

Alithea / Wait, is this not old Lady Lanterlu's bawdy house of performing girls?

Lucy / Yes, madam, and I'll wager we could find Mr Hancock in there for you.

Alithea / Away with you, impertinent girl! Well perhaps, especially considering the present circumstances, we should not be seen standing here.

[EXEUNT]

ACT V SCENE III. MR HORNER'S LODGINGS

[DOOR KNOCK, SERVANT ENTERS]

[HORNER AND MRS PINCHWIFE COME OUT OF
THE BEDCHAMBER DOOR LOOKING SLIGHTLY
DISHEVELLED]

Servant / Some ladies in masks to see you, sir.

Horner / A pox on them! They are early. Send them up, but give me a
moment to arrange things first.
[straightening his attire]

Servant / Yes, sir.

[SERVANT EXITS]

Horner / Come my dear, they must not find you here.

Mrs Pinch / (looking a satisfied woman) Who is here, dearest, dearest Mr
Horner? I care not who comes just so long as I can gaze into your
loving eyes and utter your sweet, sweet name.

[HE TAKES MRS PINCHWIFE BY THE ARM AND
GUIDES HER BACK TO THE BEDCHAMBER
DOOR]

Horner / Save your lips for later, my petite fille de joie, for now though,
you will have to hide in here until they are gone.

[HE OPENS THE DOOR AND THRUSTS HER IN
WITH A SQUEAL – CLOSING THE DOOR BEHIND
HER AS LADY GOODING, DAINTY GOODING,
AND ANITA QUIM COME INTO THE ROOM,
MASKED]

Lady G / (entering) Ah! Mr Horner, there you are. We have brought our
entertainment with us – [plonks a basket full of wine bottles on
the table] - it is our treat for you, dear toad,

Dainty / Yes, pop the cork, man. -And to allow us freedom for our merry fun, we have left Sir Jasper and old Lady Quim at home quarrelling over a game of backgammon.

Anita Quim / Yes, come on, Horner, there is an opener in the basket. Let us make the most of our time, before they notice us gone and come to interrupt us.

Lady G / Let us sit at the table then.

Horner / [opening a wine bottle] Let me lock the doors for our privacy. [cork pops]

Lady G / No, sir. Shut them only, and your lips forever. We must trust you as much as we women trust each other.

Horner / [pouring wine] You know vanity is over for me, Lady Gooding. I have no occasion for talking or boasting.

Lady G / Now, ladies, supposing we each drink two bottles of wine, then we speak the truth from our hearts.

Dainty / Agreed.

Anita Quim / Agreed.

Lady G / [Horner pours Lady Gooding's wine last] To the brim man! None of your country half measures. Truth is to be found by the brimmer and nowhere else.
(to Horner suggestively) Certainly not in your heart, false man.

[HORNER GOES AROUND THE TABLE TOPPING UP EACH GLASS OF WINE TO THE BRIM]

Horner / (aside to Lady Gooding as he tops up her glass) You have found me a true man, I'm sure.

Lady G / (aside to Horner) Not in 'every' way, thank God.
(aloud) Come, ladies. Let us sit and be merry.

Lady G / (standing to recite a verse familiar to the ladies)
Why should us poor women be forced to live
On the pittance of pleasure our damned husbands give?
So let us rejoice
With wine and with noise. To us!

[RAISES GLASS AND THEY ALL DRINK. HORNER
FILLS THE GLASSES AGAIN BETWEEN VERSES.
EACH WOMAN STANDS WHEN IT IS HER TURN
TO RECITE]

Dainty / In vain we must wake in a dull bed alone,
Whilst to our old rival, the bottle they're gone.
So put aside charms,
And lift up those arms. To us!

[THEY ALL DRINK AGAIN]

Anita Quim / 'Tis wine that gives 'em their courage and wit,
And since we're left wanting, to drink we submit.
If for beauties you'd pass,
Take a lick of the glass. To us!

[THEY ALL DRINK]

Lady G / It'll mend your complexions, for when they are gone,
He'll be lying with others, and you will get none
The best rouge we have is the red of the grape
So, sisters, drink up, to hell with good shape!

[THEY CHEER AND THEY DRINK]

[FROM THIS POINT, EVERYTIME THE WORD
'HONOUR' IS SAID A DRINK IS TAKEN BY ALL
WOMEN]

Dainty / (raises glass) Dear brimmer!
Well, in token of our openness and plain-dealing, let us throw off
our masks.

Horner / I pray it stops there, ladies, after all this wine.

Anita Quim / (raises glass) Lovely brimmer!
(gesturing towards Horner) When can I enjoy this rogue's
company at my home?

Lady G / Not till I've finished with him. I never part with a flirt till I've had
my fill of him first.
(raises glass) Dear brimmer! That which makes our husbands
short-sighted.

Dainty / And our admirers bold!   To honour!

[ALL RAISE GLASSES IN TOAST AND TAKE A
DRINK]

Anita Quim / And, for want of a flirt, a twinkle in the butler's eyes.
(to Horner) Drink, eunuch.

Lady G / Aye, Drink, surrogate husband. –Damn husbands!

Dainty / Damn men! And their vulgar ways.

Lady G / Aye, we all have reason to curse 'em and to love 'em, eh, bawdy
rogue?

Dainty / But it is so hard for a lady of quality to find a good lover, don't
you find?

Anita Quim / It seems the men would rather run the hazards of vile diseases,
than risk denial from us.

Dainty / The filthy toads choose mistresses as they do fancy clothing - for
having been fancied and worn by others.

Anita Quim / For being common and cheap.

Lady G / Whilst women of quality, like us, lie unruffled and unasked for.

Dainty / Aye, whilst the beasts change their mistresses as often as they
change their suits.

Anita Quim / And not cheap suits either.

Lady G / No. The vain fops spend more on their clothes than they do on their women. But I wonder sometimes at the depraved appetites of the men.
-Tell me, beast, when you were a man, why would you chose a club heaving with common people rather than be the only guest at a good table?

Horner / Ceremony and manners are insufferable to the sharp dressed man. The greatest hunger lies where every man is fighting for the best bit.

Lady G / (The alcohol is beginning to take effect) But I have heard that hungry men eat most heartily of another man's meat – especially if they do not have to pay for it - and let me tell you, sir, there is nowhere more free than in our houses. A person may be as free as he pleases with us, as flirtatious, as playful and as wild as he will.

Horner / I thought you all disapproved of wild men.

Lady G / Generally, that may be so, but in our flirts we desire wildness, and like wild game, well hung! He! He!

Dainty / Quite! He! He! A tame man? Foh! That is just for marrying.

Horner / But your reputations and demure expressions frightened me off.

Lady G / Our reputations! Lord, you think we women don't use our reputations as you men do? We hide behind our honour like the preacher hides behind his words, to deceive the world into trusting us. -To honour! (they drink)

Anita Quim / And that demure modesty you see in the royal boxes is as much a sign of a willing woman, as a wink in the stalls.

Lady G / You would have found us women modest only in our denials.

Horner / I beg your pardon, ladies, I was deceived by you devilishly. But why the mighty pretence of honour?

All / To honour! (they drink)

Lady G / We have told you, flirt. But sometimes it was for the same reason you men pretend business calls you away; to avoid bad company, and of course, to enjoy more privately our lovers. He! He!

Horner / Then why did you never tip me the wink?

Lady G / If truth be known, we were as much frightened by your reputation as your were by ours.

Dainty / You were so notoriously lewd.

Horner / And you were all so seemingly honourable.

Anita Quim / (beginning to slur a bit) To Honour! (they drink)

Lady G / Was that all that deterred you?

Horner / That and the expensive price to pay. You allow complete freedom to speak, you say?

Lady G / Aye, aye.

Horner / I was afraid of losing my little money.

Lady G / Money! Foh! You talk like a little fellow now. Do the likes of us expect money?

Horner / I beg your pardon, madam, but great ladies, like great merchants, set a higher price on their wares, since they are in no great need of taking the first offer.

Dainty / The likes of us putting a price on our hearts?

Anita Quim / Us? Bribed for our love? Foh!

Horner / But ladies, if you make a rendezvous, it's at a jeweller's, or a china-house, where for your 'honour to remain intact' you put a deposit on something. The poor man must pawn himself to the very limit. He pays dearly for what he takes.

Dainty / We need to be assured of our flirts' love.

Anita Quim / Love is better proven by generosity than by jealousy.

Lady G / Yes, one could be false, the other not.
-But come, here's to our flirts, (drinks) whom we must now name, and I'll begin.
This is my false rogue here.

[She claps Horner on the back]

Anita Quim / What!

Horner / (sighing) So, now it all comes out.

Lady G / Come, come. Speak, ladies. This is my false villain here.

Anita Quim / Mine too!

Dainty / And mine!

Horner / Well then, you are all three my false rogues, and there's an end to it.

Anita Quim / You said it was for me you told everyone you were no longer a man!

Dainty / You wretch! You swore to me it was for my love and honour you passed for that thing you do!

Horner / So, so.

Lady G / Wait, sister sharers! Let us not fall out. We have to take care of our honour.

Anita Quim / To honour! (hiccups)

Lady G / Oh, stuff the honour, it's all just a pretence anyway!
We may get no presents or jewels from him, but we still have our most valuable jewel – our reputation - it may be false, but it still shines brightly to an unsuspecting world.

Horner / Yes, reputation, like beauty, depends only on the opinion of others. It's as good as the real thing, provided the world thinks so.

Lady G / Well, Harry Common, I hope you can be true to three. Swear on it. Not that it's worth taking your oath on it, with your record of perjury to women.

Horner / Come, come, madam. Despite all the differences between men and women, we all perjure ourselves in a liaison, swearing to be true for as long as it lasts.

[ENTER SIR JASPER GOODING AND OLD LADY QUIM UNEXPECTEDLY]

Sir Jasper / So this is your cunning plan, Lady Gooding, to come to Mr Horner without me. You have been nowhere else, I hope.

Lady G / No, Sir Jasper.

Lady Quim / And you came straight here, Biddy?

Anita Quim / Yes, indeed, grandmother.

Sir Jasper / 'Tis well then, 'tis well. I knew once they were thoroughly acquainted with poor Mr Horner, they'd never be apart from him. (to Lady Quim) You may let her masquerade with my wife and Mr Horner, Lady Quim, I'll vouch for her reputation being safe.

[ENTER SERVANT]

Servant / Sir, there's a gentleman arrived, whom you bid me not to allow in without giving you notice. With a lady too, and other gentlemen.

Horner / Tell them to wait till I come, which shall be immediately.

Servant / Yes, sir.

[EXIT SERVANT]

Horner / You all go in there, while I send them away.

[EXIT ALL EXCEPT MR HORNER]

Horner / (aside) And now I must rid myself of the evidence.

[ONCE THEY ARE OUT THE WAY, HORNER
OPENS THE BEDROOM DOOR, AND CALLS TO
MRS PINCHWIFE]

Horner / I suspect your husband's here, he'll discover everything if you don't leave now. Quickly, I'll let you down the back way.

Mrs Pinch / But I don't know the way home, so I don't.

Horner / My servant will show you.

Mrs Pinch / No, I will stay. Are you weary of me already?

Horner / No, upon my life. To ensure our future love together, we must preserve your reputation with your husband. He'll never take you back again otherwise.

Mrs Pinch / What do I care? I don't intend to go back to him ever again. You shall be my husband now.

Horner / I can't be your husband, you are already married to him.

Mrs Pinch / You're not fooling me. I hear that London women leave their first husbands to go and live with other men every day here.

Horner / Not with me they don't.

Mrs Pinch / Pish, pshaw! You'd make me angry if I weren't so much in love with you.

Mr Pinch / (off) Where is that damn man, out of my way!

Horner / Quick, they are coming. -In my chamber again, in, I hear them.

Servant / (off) But sir, my master says wait.

[HE PUSHES MRS PINCHWIFE BACK IN THE
BEDCHAMBER WITH A SQUEAL AT SPEED]

Horner / (aside) Damn mistresses! Nothing but trouble. A man has scarce time for plunder before she has betrayed him to her husband.

[ENTER MR PINCHWIFE, ALITHEA, HANCOCK,
SPARKISH, LUCY, AND A PARSON]

Mr Pinch /   (bursting in with Alithea held by the arm)
 Come, madam, this is my witness. Since you refuse to admit it,
we'll hear it from him.
-Mr Horner, did I not bring this lady to you just now?

Horner /   Must I wrong a woman for another's sake?
But that's no new thing with me, I'm still the guilty one no matter
what I say.

Alithea /   Pray answer my brother, sir.

Horner /   I am somewhat backward in speaking of women's affairs or
disputes.

Mr Pinch /   Enough of your riddles, answer me, sir!

Alithea /   Aye, I must insist, sir, you put my brother's mind at rest.

Horner /   Then I can only say, (pauses) yes, you did bring that lady to me
just now.

Mr Pinch /   Aha!

Alithea /   What do you mean, sir? I always took you for a man of honour.

Sparkish /   So! If I had married her, she'd have made me believe the moon
had been made of Christmas pudding.

Lucy /   Now if I could speak, I could solve this riddle...

Alithea /   (interrupting) Oh, what have I done to deserve all this! You all
combining against me to ruin my honour!
(to Horner) What most concerns me now, Mr Horner, is your part
in my disgrace. It is your condemnation which I must suffer.
This troubles me more than theirs.

Hancock /   Madam, let me take care of your troubles. I will not only believe
your innocence myself, but make all the world believe it too.
-Horner, I must be concerned for this lady's honour and protect it.

Horner / I must be concerned for a lady's honour too, Hancock.

Hancock / I don't understand you.

Horner / Nor would I want you to.

Mrs Pinch / (aside, peeping from behind the door) What's the matter with
them all?

Mr Pinch / Come, come, Mr Horner. No more arguing. Here's the parson, I
didn't bring him all this way for nothing.

Hancock / Not at all, sir. I'll make use of him, if the beautiful lady, Alithea,
will allow me.

Mr Pinch / How? What do you mean, Hancock?

Sparkish / Aye, what does he mean?

Horner / I willingly surrender your sister to him, sir, he has my consent.

Mr Pinch / But he does not have mine, sir. A woman's damaged honour can
only be repaired by the man who first wronged it. So you shall
marry her now, Mr Horner, or I will have my revenge.

[MR PINCHWIFE PULLS OUT A DAGGER]

Mrs Pinch / (aside) Oh Lord, they'll kill poor Mr Horner! Besides, he shan't
marry her whilst I stand by and look on. I'll not lose my second
husband.

[RE-ENTER MRS PINCHWIFE]

Mrs Pinch / Wait!

Mr Pinch / What do I see?

Alithea / Your wife in my clothes!

Sparkish / Ha!

Mrs Pinch / Husband, please don't quarrel about finding work for the parson, he shall marry me to Mr Horner. Since now, I believe, you've had enough of me.

Horner / Damned, foolish girl!

Mrs Pinch / Please, sister, forgive me for telling so many lies of you.

Horner / I suppose the puzzle is plain now.

Lucy / No, sir, that must be my job to explain.
Good Mr Pinchwife, hear me out.

Mr Pinch / I never wish to hear women again! And I'll make sure of their silence with this-

[MR PINCHWIFE TURNS HIS DAGGER ON HIS WIFE]

Horner / No, no, not like that.

Mr Pinch / Then you shall go first, 'tis all the same to me!

[MR PINCHWIFE ADVANCES ON HORNER, BUT IS STOPPED BY HANCOCK]

Hancock / Wait!

[RE-ENTER SIR JASPER GOODING, LADY QUIM, MRS DAINTY GOODING, AND ANITA QUIM, THE LADIES CARRYING A BOTTLE & A GLASS OF WINE EACH]

Sir Jasper / What's the matter? What's the matter? Pray, what's the matter, sir? I beseech you tell me, sir.

Mr Pinch / My wife has been fu... been found communicating with him, sir, as your wife may have done too, sir, if she knows him, sir.

Sir Jasper / Pshaw, with him! ha! ha! he!

Mr Pinch / Do not mock me, sir! A cuckold is a wild beast. Have a care, sir!

Sir Jasper / No, surely you mock me, sir. He cuckold you? He can't, ha! ha! he! Why, I'll tell you, sir-

Mr Pinch / I tell you again, he has whored my wife, and yours too, if he knows her. And all the women he comes near. It's not his deception, it's his hypocrisy that ires me.

Sir Jasper / How does he deceive you? Is he a hypocrite? Wife? Sister? Is he a hypocrite?

Lady Quim / A hypocrite? A deceiver? Speak, young harlot, speak! Have you done it then?

Sir Jasper / Speak, Horner, are you a deceiver, a rogue? Have you?

Horner / So! It comes to this.

Lucy / Why don't you let me explain, Mr Horner.

Horner / Eh?

Lucy / I can get you off if she will just hold her tongue and let me explain.

Horner / (in meek desperation) You can?

Lucy / If I have good reason to.

Horner / I can give you five hundred good reasons.

Lucy / (to Horner) Done.
(to all) If you please, Mr Pinchwife, have patience to hear me, sir. I am the unfortunate cause of all this confusion. Your wife is innocent, only I am to blame. I put her up to telling you all these lies concerning my mistress, in order to break off the match between Count Sparkish and her. To make way for Mr Hancock. (she slyly winks at Hancock and slyly makes a hand sign that she expects money)

Sparkish / You did? You eternal rotten tooth! Then, it seems, my mistress was not false with me. I was only deceived by you. And my brother that should have been, is an honest man who was deceived into bringing his wife to her lover! Ha!

Lucy / I assure you, sir, she didn't come to Mr Horner out of love.

Mrs Pinch / Wait! I told lies for you, but you shall tell none for me. I love Mr Horner with all my soul, and nobody shall tell me otherwise. Please, don't go making poor Mr Horner believe anything to the contrary. 'tis spitefully done of you, I'm sure.

Horner / Quiet, you fool.

Mrs Pinch / No, I will not be quiet. (stamps foot)

[ENTER MR UPPINGTON AND DR CRACKER]

Uppington / Horner, your servant. I was with the good doctor. You must excuse our intrusion, but we heard a commotion.

Dr Cracker / For Heaven's sake, gentlemen. What is going on here?

Horner / Oh, I'm glad you've come, doctor. The hypocritical world we live in has caused this quarrel. I would had died for a crime I had not committed, and these innocent ladies would have suffered with me. To save me, pray satisfy these jealous gentlemen -that- [Whispers something to Dr Cracker]

Dr Cracker / ...Oh, I understand, is that all?
Sir Jasper, by Heavens, and upon the word of a physician, let me explain something to you, sir -[Whispers to Sir Jasper]

Sir Jasper / Oh, I see. I didn't realise they were removed with a... (looks around at the stunned expressions at his indiscretion) ...right, -Forgive me, my virtuous lady.

Lady Quim / What, then all's right again?

Sir Jasper / Aye, aye, and now let us satisfy him too. Pinchwife...
[He whispers to Mr Pinchwife]

Mr Pinch / A eunuch?

Sir Jasper / Pray sir, in confidence!

Mr Pinch / Is that what it means? You are not fooling with me?

Dr Cracker / I'll bring half the surgeons in town to swear it.

Mr Pinch / Them! They'll swear a man who lost his head in a riding accident died of a stroke.

Dr Cracker / Believe me, sir. Why, all the town has heard the news about him.

Horner / (in pretend indignation) They have?

Mr Pinch / But does all the town believe it?

Dr Cracker / Perhaps you should inquire a little. Ask these ladies.

Mr Pinch / I'm sure when I left the town, he was the lewdest fellow in it.

Dr Cracker / He has since been to France.
-Ladies and gentlemen, haven't you all heard the late sad news about poor Mr Horner?

All / Aye, aye, aye.

Uppington / Why, you jealous fool, Pinchwife. Did you doubt it? He's a total French capon.

Mrs Pinch / 'Tis false, sir, you shall not disparage poor Mr Horner, for to my certain knowledge-

Lucy / Stop, child! The pretence is over now.

Mrs Pinch / But...

Anita Quim / Someone stop her mouth!

[LADY GOODING STEPS BETWEEN MR AND MRS PINCHWIFE. LUCY STEPS BEHIND MRS PINCHWIFE WHO LEANS AROUND THE SIDE OF LADY GOODING TO CONTINUE HER REBUTTAL – SHE GETS ONE WORD IN...]

Mrs Pinch / I...

[SHE IS STOPPED SHORT AS LUCY GRABS HER
SCARF FROM BEHIND AND PULLS HER
BACKWARDS ONTO A CHAIR UNSIGHTED TO MR
PINCHWIFE AS LADY GOODING TALKS OVER
THE EPISODE)

Lady G / Upon my honour, sir, it's as true as the day is long. I know this
for certain, as I… well I put him to the test shall we say. Nothing
I did stirred him in the slightest.

Dainty / Do you think we would be seen in his company otherwise?

Anita Quim / And trust our spotless reputations with him?

Mr Pinch / Well, if this were true -but my wife- (stops confused)

Lady G / Let me have a brief word with her, Mr Pinchwife, she didn't
know.
(aside to Horner) This is what you get by trusting your secret to a
fool, Horner.
–(whispers something in Mrs Pinchwife's ear)

Alithea / Come, brother, your wife is still innocent, as you can see. You
have too strong an imagination, you know what they say, 'be
careful what you wish for'. Women and fortune are truest to
those who trust in them.

Lucy / And any wild thing grows fierce and hungry for being caged.

Alithea / (hinting for the first time that she may accept Hancock's
proposal) There's doctrine for all husbands, eh, Mr Hancock?

Hancock / I teach it, madam, so much so, that I am impatient to become one.

Uppington / And I teach by example, so I will never become one.

Sparkish / Ha! And so as not to discredit my intellect, Uppington, I'll never
become one either.

Horner / And I, alas, can't be one!

Mr Pinch / And I must be one to a country wife, with a country blight on me!

Mrs Pinch / And I must still be a country wife, I find. Because of my musty old husband I can't be a town one and do what I desire.

Horner / And now, Mr Pinchwife, I will put this day behind me by drowning myself with wine, as you should your suspicion.

Lucy / Indeed, she is innocent, sir, as I am her witness. Her aim in coming out today was to see her sister's wedding which because of your jealousy she would have missed. And what she said about her love to Mr Horner, was just innocent revenge for a husband's jealousy. Was it not, madam?

Mrs Pinch / Oh well. Since it was all lies today anyway. Yes, indeed, dearest husband, it was.

Mr Pinch / For my own sake, it would be best to just believe you all and drown my memories of the event in a barrel of wine. But... (sighs) as I find out too late, the first rule of honour is not to deceive oneself.

Lady G / (raising glass tipsily) To honour! (drinks)

Ladies / To honour!

Horner / To deceit! (raises glass, drinks)

[FINAL CURTAIN]

THE END

www.ingramcontent.com/pod-product-compliance
Lightning Source LLC
Chambersburg PA
CBHW031941260626
47157CB00016B/1833